D1137965

MALKIN'S MOUNTAIN

Wicked Malkin, jealous of the toymakers of Drüssl, plans to move the Mountain and steal all its pine trees for his new toymaking business.

How can Rudi Toymaker and his two little sons defeat Malkin, his doll-Queen, and their army of wooden soldiers, to save the heart of the Mountain and the toymakers very livelihood?

Ursula Moray Williams has written more than fifty children's books, the first of which was published in 1932. Her *Adventures of the Little Horse* has been in print for thirty-four years and is regarded as a classic. She is married and has four children and several grandchildren.

Also available by Ursula Moray Williams in Piccolo

THE THREE TOYMAKERS
THE TOYMAKER'S DAUGHTER

URSULA MORAY WILLIAMS

MALKIN'S MOUNTAIN

Cover and text illustrations by Shirley Hughes

A Piccolo Book

PAN BOOKS LTD
LONDON

First published 1948.
Revised edition published 1970
by Hamish Hamilton Children's Books Ltd.
This edition published 1972 by Pan Books Ltd,
33 Tothill Street, London, SW1.

ISBN 0 330 23312 2

Printed in Great Britain by
Cox & Wyman Ltd, London, Reading and Fakenham

CONTENTS

THE MOUNTAIN MOVES

Inside the cottage the cradle rocked to and fro on wooden rockers. The end of each rocker was carved into the shape of a face, round and wrinkled like the cheeks of little old men. When the cradle rocked the faces seemed to nod and wink in friendly grimaces that made the children laugh.

The baby slept peacefully as his mother pushed the cradle with her shoe. At the same time she was knitting jerkins for the twins, Paul and Peterkin, while her little daughter Elizabeth sat at her knee, pretending to knit too. Elizabeth's twin brothers rolled on the mat in front of the fire, wrangling over the cat.

Their Uncle Anders, who at thirteen felt himself a great deal older than all these young children, became restless as the evening shadows fell. Presently he got up to go and meet his elder brother Rudi, who was father to the family. Their mother Margaret was Rudi's wife.

Proud as he was of his young nephews and niece Anders was prouder still to be the brother of Rudi, the master toymaker of Drüssl, who had once won the King's prize for the best made toy in all the kingdom. Rudi had won the prize with a most beautiful musical box, the same that now stood in the corner of the cottage, its tunes a reward for the children when they were especially good. Small wooden figures danced on the top of it, while there seemed to be no limit to the wonderful songs that it played. Anders was as excited as the twins when Rudi took the singing box from its shelf and released its magic music.

'Take us with you to meet Father!' the twins clamoured, now, rushing after Anders.

'It is nearly supper time!' their mother warned them.

'Then we'll tell Father to hurry!' shouted Paul and Peterkin vanishing into the street.

They followed Anders past the darkening houses, along the track to the foot of the great Mountain beyond, where Rudi Toymaker had gone to fetch new timber for the making of his toys.

There were no fir trees in the kingdom so fine as those growing on the mountainside above the village of Drüssl. The Mountain stood, half in the King's lands, and half in the kingdom beyond. The border between the two countries was on the mighty summit, beyond which the fir trees ran down to different villages and their pastures. What use these villages made of their trees nobody knew, since the Mountain towered between the two kingdoms. People in country districts do not trouble much about things going on elsewhere.

At the foot of the Mountain, on the Drüssl side, flowed a sparkling stream, crossed by stepping stones that at present were covered with water.

The little boys amused themselves by splashing from stepping-stone to stepping-stone, admiring Anders, whose longer legs could cross the stream at a stride.

'Our Anders can do anything!' Paul said to Peterkin. 'Whistle up the fishes, Uncle Anders!'

Anders whistled, and whether by chance or by curiosity, the little fishes darted out of the stones and escaped into the shadows.

Paul and Peterkin snatched at them in vain, while Anders reached down more quietly. Suddenly there were three in the palm of his hand.

'Our Anders can do anything he likes!' shouted Peterkin. 'Call up the owls, Uncle Anders!'

Anders put his hands to his mouth and made strange noises. At once an owl called back from the high Mountain. It was Rudi, who recognized his young brother's voice, but the twins grew round-eyed with admiration.

'Now call the wind, Anders!'

Anders whistled low, mysteriously, and they could hear the sighing of the pine trees answering him.

'Can you do everything, Uncle Anders?' the twins asked in awe.

'Everything!' he told them solemnly.

'Can you move a mountain?' demanded Peterkin.

A little taken aback, Anders replied: 'Certainly, on the right day.'

'When is the right day, Uncle Anders?'

'Who knows?'

'How can you tell?'

'Only by trying.'

'Do you often try?'

'Not very often.'

'Are there many right days, or only one?'

'Only one.'

'Might it be today?'

'It might, but it isn't likely.'

'Do try, Uncle Anders!'

For a long time Anders stood staring gravely at the mountain, while Paul and Peterkin held their breath. Their fingers twitched with excitement.

At last Anders shook his head, and was about to speak when there came a mighty trembling under his feet, as if the very roots of the Mountain were loosening themselves down in the bed of the stream. Cracks, inches wide, appeared on the farther bank, and as they stared they saw the stream-bed had widened by several feet, as if the Mountain had withdrawn its roots from it. The water now flowed muddy and shallow, while the stepping-stones were uncovered and the little frightened fishes fled from sight.

As they stood transfixed by amazement – the twins triumphant and Anders in a daze, Rudi Toymaker came striding down to join them, his face pale against the tree trunk that he carried.

'The Mountain is moving!' he cried.

2

THE STRANGER AND THE
SINGING BOX

After supper that evening the children begged for a tune
from the singing box that Rudi had made for the King's
prize.

The twins could talk of nothing but the mysterious
tremor they had felt on the mountainside. Their mother
wanted them to go to bed, for she could see that their
father looked anxious and disturbed. But the boys were
so over-excited that Rudi fetched the singing box to distract them, and was about to wind it up when there
came a rat-tat at the door.

Anders opened the door to a tall, bearded traveller
with blue eyes and shabby clothes, who lifted his staff in
greeting as he asked in a ringing voice:

'Is this the house of the toymakers of Drüssl?'

'It is!' Rudi replied.

'It is!' came an aged voice from the next room, as old
Peter Toymaker, who had adopted Rudi as a boy and
taught him his trade, came slowly through the doorway.
An old man now, he lived contentedly in the back-
ground with his memories, among which was the prize
he had shared with Rudi at the time of the King's contest. Old Peter had made a furnished dolls' house so like

any of the real houses in Drüssl that people still talked about it.

Nowadays he seldom spoke to anyone outside his beloved family, but this evening to their surprise, he walked

across the room with some of his old dignity and firmness to welcome the stranger.

'What news have you brought for the toymakers of Drüssl, traveller?' he asked.

The stranger bowed low before replying, and at once old Peter led him to the fire, where Margaret put into his hands a bowl of hot soup, so it was some little while before he began to tell them the grave news that he had learnt on his journey.

Even the twins and their sister Elizabeth could understand something of the matters he was talking about. They had often heard the story of the King's contest, and knew that the prize had been nearly won by a wicked rival toymaker called Malkin, from the neighbouring village of Pils. He had made a doll so beautiful and so lifelike that she had almost carried away the prize, in fact the King was about to award it to her master when her wickedness betrayed her, for Malkin had never made a really perfect thing. When the King discovered how basically unworthy the pair of them were, he banished them from his kingdom for ever, and shared the prize between Rudi and Peter Toymaker.

From that day on Malkin and his doll Marta had never been heard of again.

But now the traveller had a strange tale to tell of a master toymaker in the next kingdom who was possessed of magic powers. He had set up a new toymaking business which he meant to make the greatest in the world, the stranger said. And he had set an army of toy wooden soldiers with wooden guns and cannons to protect all the pine trees that grew on his own side of the Mountain, so that nobody should take one away.

'But there are thousands of pine trees!' Rudi said scornfully. 'Those on this side will last me and my children and my children's children all our lives for toymaking, and all the toymakers in Drüssl too. What is more, while we cut down the old trees the new ones are growing. They will last us forever I believe!'

'Ah Master Toymaker! Don't speak so rashly!' cried the traveller. 'Do you realize that this very same Malkin is planning to do you a mischief? He has heard of your success and your fame and is bitterly jealous of the toy-makers of Drüssl! He plans to steal all your trees, Master Rudi Toymaker! How he will do it I cannot say, but I am sure it is true.'

'That is against the law!' said Anders angrily. 'The King's soldiers will protect our trees and chase out any wooden soldier that dares to come across our bound-ary!'

'Ah!' said Rudi, suddenly comprehending. 'But sup-posing that the boundary moved?'

'The Mountain is moving! We saw it!' piped up the twins. 'Anders told it to and the Mountain moved!'

'Not Anders, but some evil power moved the Moun-tain.' Rudi murmured. 'So, neighbour Malkin – if this is your doing—! You would rob us of our pine trees, would you? We shall see about that!'

Little Elizabeth who was nodding asleep on old Peter's knee, now woke up and began to plead for the promised tune from the singing box, and as her brothers too began to clamour their father took out his key, and with a word of apology to the stranger, placed the sing-ing box on a bench.

The sleepy children sat up expectantly, the grown-ups relaxed, and the box began to sing. The wonder of the box was that no one knew what it would play next. Sometimes it was a favourite dance, and sometimes a tune from long ago that seemed to have been left for-gotten at the bottom of the box for ages past.

Tonight, when it had played something that pleased

each member of the family, it suddenly began a song
that none of them had heard before, so sad and plaintive
that it stirred all their hearts. And with the music came
words, as sorrowful as the tune:

'The Mountain is moving!
The Mountain is leaving us!
Soon. Oh! soon the Mountain will be gone!
What evil power is taking away our pine trees?
Who will defeat the wicked one; the conqueror?
Who will be brave enough to save our Mountain?

Only he who conquers the beat of the heart of
*   the Mountain,*
Only he who outwits the guile of the beautiful
*   stranger,*
He alone who leaves his home and his cradle
*   fatherless.'*

Margaret gave a little cry and clutched her baby.
Rudi looked sternly into the fire. The two older men
shook their heads.

'Those are strange words to sing. Better forget
them!' said old Peter Toymaker.

'But who is the beautiful stranger?' Anders said,
bursting out laughing. 'Surely it can't be Malkin?'

'They say the wicked toymaker has a Queen in his
country who is half-doll and half-child, and that she is
very beautiful,' said the traveller. 'Everyone obeys
her, even where they will not obey the toymaker himself. I have never set eyes on her. I didn't like what I
saw of the country so I did not loiter in the place. But
I do beg of you sirs, to pay attention to what I say, and
to take warning.'

3

THE WOODEN SOLDIER

Long after the younger ones were gone to bed their elders sat discussing the terrible news that the stranger had brought.

Anders did his best to listen to their conversation through the floorboards, but he could not stay awake for long, and when he opened his eyes it was broad morning, the twins were struggling into their clothes and the stranger gone on his way.

That day Rudi called together all the men of the village and told them of the stranger's warning.

'If this is true we shall all lose our trades and be ruined!' he said. 'Not only we toymakers but you, John Carpenter and you, Master Coffinmaker, and you, Bernard Barrowmender. If the pine trees go, so will our work and all our families will starve. Now, I have thought of a plan by which we may help ourselves. We believe that Malkin may be trying to move the Mountain, but the village he cannot move, because the little stream that runs round the foot of the Mountain protects it. Magic cannot act through running water. Before he has time to move all the pine trees into his own boundaries we must cut down as many as possible and store them here in the village!'

Rudi's neighbours raised a cheer when they heard his

plan. At once they ran home to fetch their saws and sharpen their axes, but when they returned their wives, mothers, sisters and sweethearts came too, all sobbing and protesting at the danger that lay waiting up the Mountain for their men.

'You yourself told us there were toy soldiers with cannons at the summit!' they reproached Rudi. 'We shall never see any of you again!'

'And what do *you* say, sweetheart?' Rudi asked his wife Margaret, who had joined the other women with her baby in her arms.

Margaret put a hand in his and spoke bravely to the other women.

'I think we ought to be proud of our men!' she said. 'If we let Malkin have his way we shall lose our homes and all they mean to us. Malkin means to ruin the people of Drüssl by taking away their livelihood, and if we keep our husbands at home he will do so all the more quickly. Let us send them out with our blessing and pray for their safe return!'

Margaret was a favourite in the village and the other women stopped protesting. If a few anxious tears were shed at the men's departure they were hastily wiped away as Rudi and his neighbours tramped out of the village and up the mountainside.

The schoolchildren had a holiday, for even the schoolmaster had fetched his axe and joined the rest. 'Where shall I get my desks and benches and of what shall I make my cane if there are no more pine trees?' he asked.

Anders tried to go with Rudi, but his brother ordered him to stay at home and take his own place in looking after Margaret, so the whole day long he cut firewood, spread the washing on the grass to dry, and peeled potatoes, while high above on the Mountain the *tap-tap-tap* of the axes sounded. They heard no echo of shot or sounds of cannon-balls.

In the evening the chopping ceased, and every woman and child who could leave a cradle or a cooking pot to look after itself, ran to the stream to meet the returning woodsmen.

When they arrived there they were appalled to find the bed of the stream was now so wide and shallow one might have built a house upon it. The banks on the further side were so crumbled and cracked that you could see for yourself the agony with which the Mountain had withdrawn its foundations. The little fishes had fled, and the twins searched for them in vain. The stepping stones were quite dry.

But while they were staring the men came tramping down the mountainside, each carrying a tree-trunk on his shoulders, and at the sight of them all safe and unharmed the women forgot the empty stream-bed. The procession returning to the village was like a festival, with the children throwing garlands of flowers on to the great pine logs that were piled behind the burgomaster's house, the first of the store to come.

When he arrived home, and was sitting with a twin on either knee, Rudi told his family of the day's adventures.

His plan had been to first cut down the pines from the very top of the Mountain so that as many as possible might be saved before Malkin moved them across the border. He led his band of men to a great height and left them felling while he climbed to the top to see what was going on there.

At first he saw nothing at all.

Then he noticed that the rocky ridge marking the King's boundary had already moved a little beyond the summit. The peak of the Mountain now lay in the next kingdom, and even as he watched it a tremor shook the earth and with his own eyes he saw the Mountain move.

Suddenly a dozen small wooden soldiers bobbed up from the rocks that lined the boundary. A toy cannon fell off a ledge and landed on its back. Two soldiers immediately scrambled down to fetch it, and set it up again.

When they saw Rudi they pointed the cannon directly at him, jumping and jabbering and threatening him with their muskets.

'Do not fire!' Rudi called out, 'I am not going to cross your boundary! I am only going to cut down one or two trees on our own side of the border and take them home!'

The little wooden soldiers at once put down their guns

and watched curiously while Rudi stepped boldly into the open – slung his jacket on the bough of a tree and set to work with his axe.

When the tree came thundering down the wooden soldiers laughed and clapped their hands. The men working below heard the tree fall and came up to watch. The wooden soldiers stared but did not attempt to fire on them. It seemed they had been told not to shoot at anyone who remained on the King's side of the border, and every time a tree fell they laughed and jumped with delight.

Now and then a mighty shudder shook the Mountain and the men of Drüssl looked at one another. Nobody spoke but they set to work with new vigour so that the trees toppled and crashed on every side of them.

At last it was time to go home, and when Rudi put his coat on he found, hiding behind it, one of the little wooden soldiers who had strayed across the border and was either too stupid or too curious to go back. The small wooden figure stood no higher than Rudi's knee and was comically carved and painted. As he picked it up the wooden legs and arms hung down foolishly, the round eyes stared.

'This will make a playfellow for the twins!' said Rudi putting the soldier into the large pocket of his coat.

Old Peter Toymaker was interested to see the wooden puppet. He examined it very carefully.

'This is Malkin's work!' he said. 'I have seen it before.'

'So have I!' said Anders. 'When I was a little boy I used to look in his shop window at Pils, and I remember his puppets very well. They were all grinning and

squinting just like this one. Look at the way his tongue
sticks out! He is frightening Elizabeth!'

But the twins, Paul and Peterkin, were enchanted

with their new toy who shouldered arms, stood at attention or at ease and did everything that he was told to do.
They drilled him from morning till night and taught
him to salute and to make his bow to their sister
Elizabeth.

But she never overcame her dislike of the puppet, unlike the baby, who showed no fear of it at all, but banged him ceaselessly against the side of the cradle, holding him first by one leg and then by the other.

4

ANDERS LAYS A TRAP

The twins, Paul and Peterkin, wrangled so incessantly over the wooden puppet that the only solution was to take it away from them whenever the quarrelling broke out.

'I wish Rudi had never brought it home to you!' Anders said crossly, tossing the soldier on to a high shelf beside the cuckoo clock for the fifth time one morning. 'You never quarrelled so much before you had it.'

'But Paul tells it to stand at ease when I say *shun*!' Peterkin wailed. 'Then it falls down all in a heap and won't do anything at all!'

'If Father had brought us *two* puppets we shouldn't have anything to quarrel about!' Paul said sagely. 'Do get us another one next time you go up the mountain, Uncle Anders!'

Now that all seemed safe on the Drüssl side of the border Anders was sometimes allowed to go tree felling with the other men. In fact every pair of hands was needed, for the Mountain's movements became more violent every day. The bed of the stream was now a wide and stony desert. Fresh chasms appeared on the Mountain's slopes every morning, while strange subterranean rumbles filled the air.

But the pile of timber behind the burgomaster's house grew steadily higher, and now the empty slopes at the summit of the Mountain where the trees had been felled could be plainly seen from the village street. There was to be a feast and a celebration in the village on the day the thousandth pine was felled. Margaret and all her neighbours were already baking for it.

When Anders promised to find another puppet for the twins their mother reproved him sharply.

'Now we shall have no peace at all!' she scolded. 'If you don't find them another soldier we shall never hear the end of it, and if we do they will have two puppets to fight about instead of one.'

Anders tossed off the warning of his sister-in-law and basked in the adulation of his nephews. They were so sure he could do anything he wished to do. Catching another puppet was a simple affair compared with moving a mountain!

The soldiers on the summit no longer chattered or shouted when the pine trees fell. They remained very silent, watching the men from behind the rocks.

Anders tried to talk to them on the first day he was allowed to go with the rest of the men to the Mountain, but when he went too close, they began to man their wooden cannons, so he gave it up.

On the Drüssl side there were trolls and goblins living on the lower slopes. Anders had made friends with them when he was young, and he still saw them from time to time.

Now he began to construct a wooden sentry-box, with a door that closed with a string like a trap.

It was a very smart box, painted green and white,

quite a palace of a box for a wooden soldier. Anders attached a long piece of string to the door.

Then he walked out to the lower slopes of the Mountain, carrying the box under his arm.

The trolls and goblins knew Anders' voice and came to his whistle. When he had welcomed them and told them how pleased he was to see them again he explained what he wanted them to do.

'We don't go up to the top of the Mountain any longer!' the trolls objected.

'It is too far, and the box is too heavy!' the goblins said.

'We don't like the wooden soldiers!' added the trolls. 'They are stealing our mountain away, those people over there! They have changed the beat of its heart and are turning it to stone. When the whole of the Mountain is over the border its heart will stop beating and be hard as rock, for ever. Everything on this side of it will die, whatever you may say. Tell Rudi to be very careful!'

Anders listened attentively to their warning but he still begged the goblins and the trolls to take his sentry-box to the top of the Mountain and to put it where the wooden soldiers could see it in the morning.

'I will come with you to see that they do you no harm,' he promised, and at last they agreed to help him.

With three or four leading the way carrying the sentry-box, they climbed together high, high to where the pine trees ended and the stumps began. There were now a thousand stumps on the mountainside, for the thousandth tree had been cut and the men were taking a well-earned holiday. That same evening a big feast and

celebration would be held in the village of Drüssl.

Where the pine trees ended Anders stopped. He did not want the wooden soldiers to see him, so he lurked among the pine boles while the goblins carried the box forward, placing it just inside the King's boundary beside some rocks. Then they scuttled back towards the trees, too terrified to look behind them.

But the wooden soldiers were much too inquisitive to fire at them. They had never seen a sentry-box before and thought it was a present brought by the trolls and goblins – so new and neat and shining.

Anders' hand trembled on the end of the long piece of string attached to the door. He watched the little soldiers swarming over the border to crowd around the box, until the biggest and the bravest stepped inside.

At once Anders jerked his string. The door closed with a snap on its prisoner, and while the rest of the soldiers hurried back to man their guns Anders pulled the sentry-box towards him. Then away he ran down the mountainside with the trolls and goblins scampering at his heels while a volley of popguns and cannon-balls rang out behind him, much too far away to do him any harm.

Anders was highly pleased with himself when he opened the kitchen door and stepped inside.

Margaret was packing her cakes and rolls into a basket. She did not at all welcome the dejected puppet that Anders tipped out on to the floor. But the twins, dressed for the feast in their best blue jackets with silver buttons, were delighted.

'The new one is mine!' said Peterkin immediately.

'No *mine*!' said Paul. 'Yours is the old one!'

'There! They are at it again!' said Anders, as his nephews fought and scuffled on the floor.

'What did I tell you?' cried Margaret, pulling them apart and dusting down their jackets.

'I thought we might get a little peace!' said Anders crestfallen, angry that nobody had congratulated him on his cunning.

Rudi came in wearing his Sunday suit. He tossed both puppets on to the high shelf beside the cuckoo clock, where they huddled together, limp and dejected, as the family left the cottage for the feast. Rudi and Margaret led the way, carrying the baby in turns, and old Peter Toymaker came last of all, holding little Elizabeth by the hand.

5

THE REVENGE OF THE
WOODEN PUPPETS

The cottage was very quiet when the family had gone to the feast. The cradle was empty, and the rockers still.

Dancing in the sunbeams were thousands and thousands of dust specks, whirled into the air by the twins' last rough-and-tumble. Margaret was not there to chase them so they slowly settled on the chairs and table, on the cuckoo clock and on the painted helmets of the two puppets nodding on the shelf.

The cuckoo bounced out of his little house to announce six o'clock. 'Cuckoo!' he shouted six times banging the door shut in the middle of the last 'Cuck—!'

The puppets stirred.

'Our Master, Malkin Toymaker, made a clock just like that once,' one said to the other. 'He sent it as a present to a lady who had displeased him. Every hour it called the time so sweetly, but at every thirteenth hour out popped a toad!'

Both puppets rocked with laughter.

'*Koo!*' screamed the cuckoo, his conscience pricking him. Bang went the door. Both little men sprang to attention and shivered with fright for the next half-hour.

'What's happening up the Mountain?' the first whispered some time later.

'The men from Drüssl are clearing the trees away so fast!' the second answered. 'Malkin is furious! The Mountain has moved a great way but he hasn't captured any pine trees yet – only stumps! If these people can store enough timber in the village for their needs, then all Master's magic will have worked in vain!'

'I don't give a fig for Malkin!' the first puppet said. 'But the Queen is another matter. The day you were taken away from us, brother, she came up the Mountain and begged us to do all we could, for her sake. She said if we captured the Mountain she would be the richest Queen in the world and she would make us all her Generals. She is so beautiful. I would do all I could to please her!'

'Well we can't do anything about it here on this shelf!' said the second puppet. 'We are prisoners and the people of Drüssl have cut down a thousand pine trees and are celebrating as if Malkin was already beaten at his game!'

'Listen! I have a plan!' the first puppet whispered. He put his wooden face close to his companion's ear, and what he said was so startling that the little soldier's eyes grew round with excitement. His wooden musket rattled at his side.

'Where is it? Where is it?' he asked.

'Hush! Don't let the cuckoo hear what we are saying! Look! It is down there on the floor under the cradle where I saw him drop it. Go and get it and bring it back to me!'

'It is a long way to the floor, brother!'

'Pooh! What's that to a wooden soldier? You can climb down the cuckoo's chains. I would go myself only I have been so bruised and banged about by the baby and those tiresome little boys that I am all covered with bruises. Don't tell me you are afraid to climb down, a brave wooden soldier like you?'

The second puppet noticed that it was almost time for the cuckoo to call the next quarter of an hour. It would never do to be caught sliding down the chains at such a moment. He waited until the bird had bobbed out and gone in again. The cuckoo noticed the puppets staring at him and thought they looked sly. Stupid, clumsy things!

he said to himself, vain of his own finely carved house and painted feathers. Bang! went his little door.

The second wooden soldier gingerly slipped from the shelf and slid down the clock chain. The cuckoo took no notice, if he felt it at all. Often the mice ran up and down his chains, or the children twitched at them. All his life went on inside his house, thinking and dreaming. None of his dreams were more than a quarter of an hour long.

The wooden soldier scampered across the floor and picked up something that was lying under the baby's cradle. It was Rudi's tinder-box! The puppet waved it triumphantly at his companion before climbing up the chains again. They hid the box between them on the shelf.

Some time later Rudi and his family came home. The twins clamoured for their puppets, but as they were very tired after the feast Margaret undressed them and put them to bed, to the great relief of the little wooden men. Rudi hunted everywhere for his tinder-box but he did not think of looking on the shelf.

'You must have dropped it at the feast!' Margaret told him. 'Somebody is sure to pick it up and bring it to you in the morning.'

The whole family went to bed, while outside the moon rose to shine proudly over the thousand felled pine trees stacked up behind the burgomaster's house.

When the cuckoo called eleven times the two soldiers stirred again.

'Is it time?' said one.

'Not yet!' said the other. 'Wait till midnight!' so they went to sleep again for a whole hour.

Midnight came. Twelve times the cuckoo called, and when he had banged his door for the last time the two puppets climbed off the shelf and slid down the chains, carrying with them Rudi's tinder-box. They stole across the kitchen floor, climbed on a chair and began to open the door.

'The mice are very lively tonight!' the cuckoo thought, feeling his chains vibrate. He bounced out with an extra 'Cuckoo!' for luck, to scare them away. The first puppet had turned the key while the second pushed open the door. They were so startled by the cuckoo's noise that between them they dropped the tinder-box.

The cuckoo heard it tinkle. He saw them pick it up and scamper outside as fast as their wooden legs would carry them. He paused half-in and half-outside his little wooden door.

'This is very odd!' he said to himself, 'I heard Rudi hunting half the evening for his tinder-box and here are these little wooden men running away with it!' Restless and uneasy he did not shut the door but continued to watch and listen, wondering what the meaning of all this could be.

Meanwhile the wooden soldiers had hurried into Rudi's workshop at the back of the cottage and were filling their arms with chips, shavings and anything they could find which was likely to burn. Carrying their burdens they staggered down the village street, keeping in the shadows and dodging from house to house until they reached the burgomaster's field. There the pile of stately pine trunks shone like silver in the moonlight.

The wicked puppets thrust their bundles of kindling

underneath the pile and pushed Rudi's tinder-box into the shavings. Click! and with a crackle first a tiny coil of smoke and then a bright flame sprang skywards. Another followed and then another and another . . .

'What a bonfire! What a bonfire!' chuckled the puppets. 'Perhaps Master will see the blaze across the Mountain and will guess what we are doing!'

'We will get promotion!' said the other puppet. 'We may even be decorated by the Queen and raised to her bodyguard! Long live Malkin and the Queen of the Mountains! Long live Malkin Toymaker and our beautiful Queen!'

Inside the cottage the cuckoo grew more and more restless.

He heard the puppets chuckling as they carried the kindling from Rudi's workshop, and felt that something was very wrong.

'Cuckoo!' he called. 'Cuckoo! Cuckoo! Cuckoo!'

Old Peter Toymaker, sleeping the light fitful sleep of the very old, heard the cuckoo's frantic note. 'The bird is crazy!' he said to himself. 'Rudi will have to see to him in the morning. He has only just struck midnight and there he goes again!'

'Cuckoo! Cuckoo!' the little bird still called.

Old Peter stirred restlessly. His night was spoiled. If the bird did not stop shouting he would not sleep till morning. He rapped on the wall with his stick.

'Anders! Go and tell Rudi the clock has gone crazy! The bird is calling all hours and I cannot go to sleep!'

But Rudi was deeply asleep after soothing Elizabeth who had had nightmares following the speeches and so

many good things to eat. He could not be roused.

'I'll go and lock the cuckoo in his house myself!' Anders called through the wall. He went into the kitchen and pushed the little bird firmly behind his painted doors. Then he bolted the tiny shutters and ran back to bed. The night was short enough without spending half of it in chasing wooden cuckoos.

But back in bed sleep did not come quickly. Something puzzled him and filled his thoughts. How did it happen that the kitchen was full of moonlight when Margaret always drew the curtains so tightly? And surely he had not dreamed it – wasn't the door to the street ajar?

And now he remembered that the shelf beside the cuckoo clock was empty. Where were the wooden puppets, since the twins had not been allowed to take them to bed? At the same time he heard the cuckoo struggling behind its painted doors. What was the matter with the bird? Had it lost its senses?

Once more, Anders got out of bed and ran into the kitchen, where a glance through the window showed him a terrible sight. Down the street behind the burgomaster's house flames rose scarlet, yellow and gold in a leaping pillar of whirling sparks and light.

'Rudi! Rudi!' Anders called at the top of his voice, running out of the house in his nightshirt and bare feet. 'Come quickly! Quickly! The pine trees are alight!'

The wooden soldiers did not wait to witness the success of their plan. When they saw that the pile was well alight they ran off towards the Mountain as fast as their wooden legs would carry them, never looking back until they were safe among the pine trees.

Once there they fell into line, shouldered their muskets, and marched upwards to report themselves to their commander and receive their reward.

Anders shouted: 'Fire! Fire!' all the way down the village street. Everyone had gone to bed, tired out from the feast, but Anders' cries and the roaring of the burning trees soon roused them. Heads popped out of every window.

Men, women and children poured into the street carrying pails, jugs, anything that would hold water, as they ran towards the fire.

The burgomaster with a white and stricken face was already on the scene. Rudi came with two pails followed by old Peter Toymaker carrying another, his step as swift as Rudi's in his anxiety.

The burgomaster drilled the people into a chain that stretched from the village pump to the blazing pine trees. Buckets of water were passed from hand to hand, every man, woman and child working their hardest, heedless of blisters or aching limbs as they fought to save their property.

The burgomaster's house was threatened by flying sparks but he would not have water wasted on it. 'Let it go! What does the house matter, if we can save the trees?' he said.

The house did not burn but the blaze was so tremendous that before it the moon paled and wilted. Rudi imagined Malkin gloating as he watched the glow in the sky from the far side of the Mountain. Too late he blamed himself for not setting a guard over the pine trees. No thought of treachery had ever crossed his mind, and where the blow had come from he did not know.

Suddenly he heard a cheer from the chain of men, and raising his head from his toil saw that the blaze was dying down. A dense cloud of smoke was taking the place of the flames while the stars began to wink again in the far night sky.

Little by little the fire was conquered; the smoke rolled away, the flames and ashes hissed into silence. The great monument of charred timber stood at last four-square in the moonlight, glittering with water, scorched to more than half its height, but nevertheless saved.

Exhausted as they were, Rudi and the burgomaster would not rest until they had made a count of all the trunks that had been rescued. More than a quarter of their labours had been completely destroyed. Many more were charred, but if it had not been for Anders' timely warning the whole thousand might have been lost and the burgomaster's house as well.

'It was Uncle Peter who woke me, and the cuckoo clock woke Uncle Peter!' Anders said. He ran back to let the little bird out of its prison.

'From now on one of us must keep guard over the trees every night,' Rudi said. 'And we must work an hour longer every day to make up for the timber we have lost. I don't think this will be Malkin's last attempt to ruin us and we shall have to keep our wits about us.'

In the morning Paul and Peterkin asked for their wooden puppets.

Anders tracked their footprints as far as the foot of the Mountain, where he found Rudi's tinder-box lying where they had dropped it in their flight. There was no further sign of them and they were never seen in the kingdom again.

However, Anders noticed that there were several new cracks up on the mountainside. Some of them resembled chasms.

6

DISAPPEARANCE OF RUDI

The threat to the trees and the loss of so many of them had changed Rudi from a cheerful and optimistic fellow to a morose and gloomy one. He blamed himself for not taking proper precautions against the disaster. He spent his evenings gazing silently into the fire. The children hardly dared speak to him, and the singing box was locked away.

Every morning Rudi was first on the Mountain with his axe, and Margaret waited until darkness to hear his step again. The other men described how he worked by himself, at a distance from them, sparing himself nothing, felling two trees to their one. In spite of his withdrawal they still trusted and loved him.

'Once all the trees are cut down Rudi will be happy again!' Anders told Margaret to comfort her.

Meanwhile the Mountain daily groaned and shuddered, slipping little by little into Malkin's kingdom. Anders very seldom went with the men now. For the most part of the time he had to take his brother's place in looking after the family at home.

One night they waited anxiously for Rudi to come, as for once they had good news to tell him.

A parcel had arrived from the city, where Rudi and Anders' sister Elsa was a successful dressmaker. She even

made clothes for the King and Queen. The parcel contained presents for everybody, an embroidered apron for Margaret, toys, cakes, sweets and apples for the twins, a knife for Anders, a pretty dress for Elizabeth, a cap for the baby, and a hunter's horn for Rudi.

'Now we shall always know when he is coming home!' said Anders. 'We will tell him to blow it when he has cut down his last tree and then we can tell when to expect him!'

Margaret smiled happily, while the twins blew fearsome noises on the new horn. Anders laid out a feast with the apples, cakes, fruit and sweets Elsa had sent. Elizabeth begged to wear her new dress to show her father. Old Peter Toymaker put on the velvet slippers that had been his share of the parcel and the cottage became full of excitement and anticipation. Paul and Peterkin ran to the door every other minute to see if Rudi were in sight, but still he did not come.

It grew dark, and the twins looked longingly at the cakes and apples. Old Peter Toymaker fell asleep in his chair.

'There won't be any more of this waiting and watching once Rudi has his horn!' said Anders. 'We shall hear it all over the village!'

The cuckoo called nine o'clock. Margaret gave an apple to each twin and slipped the new dress off sleepy Elizabeth. She put the child's nightdress on and tucked her up in bed. A little later she put the twins to bed too, protesting a little, but with a cake in each hand.

Anders whittled at a piece of wood with his new knife, listening for Rudi's step and pretending to be quite unconcerned. When Margaret had gone upstairs to tuck up the children he opened the door and stood for a long time looking up at the Mountain in the darkness.

Old Peter woke, feeling the draught from the door.

'Where is Rudi?' he said at once.

'He'll be here in a minute,' Anders replied, as Margaret came into the room.

But Rudi did not come.

Margaret and Anders hung a lantern outside the door and sat up all night to wait for him. Old Peter slept and woke in turns, certain that his dear, adopted son would return before morning. But Rudi did not come back to the cottage that night.

Early the next day the whole village knew about his disappearance. Calling out messages of comfort to Margaret the men set out in a band to find him, convinced that he had fallen and hurt his leg or been in some way prevented from making his way home.

'We will bring him back!' they shouted as they passed the cottage. Margaret was greatly comforted and set to work on her usual household duties, quite sure that Rudi would soon be found and brought back to her.

Anders went with the men. He had promised to blow three loud blasts on Rudi's new horn when they found his brother, but the three blasts never came.

In the evening the men came home solemn and disheartened, and they did not bring Rudi with them. Led by the burgomaster they entered Margaret's house to tell her they had searched every inch of the Mountain in vain. Neither Rudi nor his axe were anywhere to be found.

'But there are great chasms leading down to the very heart of the Mountain and running in all directions,' the men said. 'He may have fallen down one of these and be lying at the bottom. We shall go and look again in the morning.'

But although they searched all the next day and the next and the one after that they did not find a trace of Rudi. Meanwhile the Mountain shuddered and moved. New crevices opened, sometimes at the searchers' very feet. A pale mist began to shroud the lower slopes, so that the summit, which had moved far into Malkin's territory, was seldom seen.

At last the other women in the village refused to allow their men to go and cut down more pine trees. They were afraid that they too would disappear inside the Mountain for ever. Only Anders went back there every day, and sometimes, in spite of their mother's fears, the twins followed him.

All three of them were determined to find Rudi and to bring him safely home. They refused to believe that he was dead, or lost to them forever. Old Peter Toymaker looked anxious and careworn these days, but he too was certain that Rudi was still alive.

'One day he will come back to us!' he said, nodding his white head.

But the days dragged wearily.

7

THE HEART OF THE MOUNTAIN

All this time Rudi Toymaker was much nearer to his family than they had any idea of. He was a prisoner inside the Mountain, and his escape was guarded on every hand.

Rudi's heart was heavy on that bright autumn morning when he climbed the mountainside, for he could not shed the burden of guilt he felt at the loss of their precious timber. Until with his own hands he had made up the number of trees they had lost he knew he would never feel lighthearted again. That was the reason he worked apart from the others and why he was so silent and sad in his home. And although the pile of pine boles was growing bigger again, much of it by his own efforts, his spirits remained low, until on this beautiful morning a little bird fluttered out of the bracken, singing, and the words it sang were only for Rudi:

> *'O Rudi Toymaker!*
> *Where is your courage?*
> *Take heart!*
> *Take heart!*
> *Go back and laugh with your children once again!*
> *Salute your neighbours with a smile!*
> *All your friends look to you for help.*

You are their leader, Rudi Toymaker!
Show them you have courage!
Show them you are strong!
Go back to them!
Go back! Go back!
Better lose a thousand trees than break a brave man's
heart!'

Suddenly Rudi's sore heart was filled with fresh hope and gratitude to the little bird fast disappearing into the sky. The bird was right. He was shutting out his family and his friends in his grief, just when they needed him most. Today he would work side by side with his neighbours again. Then in the evening he would laugh and play games with his children and perhaps they would have a tune from the singing box.

But as he stood there with a smile of new confidence on his face the Mountain shook with a terrible trembling. A chasm opened under his feet, presenting a yawning fissure that engulfed him before he could spring aside or save himself with a thrust of his axe.

Down, down Rudi fell into the heart of the Mountain — to the very bottom of the great pit Malkin had prepared for him, and while the little bird still sang, high in the clouds above, Rudi lay on the dark rocks below, unconscious, with the shaft of his broken axe still clasped in his hand.

It was a long time before he opened his eyes and realized where he was.

Far above him the daylight glimmered like a distant star. Around him, the chasm was lighted by that faint

mountain light that is half fairy and half natural. He
stirred and groaned a little, feeling his bruises and his
aching head. But no arms or legs were broken, and in a
little while he was able to sit up, and then to stagger to
his feet and look about him.

He had fallen into a narrow passage that ran on deep

inside the Mountain. As he took a step forward a dozen
little wooden soldiers stepped silently out of the shadows,
falling in escort about him with bayonets fixed. He could
see it would be foolish to try to resist them, for his axe
was broken in two places, so he allowed himself to be
marched away down the passage, aching and weary and
wondering what fate awaited him at the other end.

After a while the passage grew broader and lighter, as
the dim mountain light was quenched by many lanterns
hanging along the roof. Each lantern was decorated by a
fearsome mask that gave a sinister welcome to their
coming.

The passage opened out into a magnificent pillared
hall topped by a dome. This too was well illuminated
and a thousand moving puppet people circled and re-

circled the floor, all dressed in gaily painted coats and dresses. This place must be the very centre of the Mountain, Rudi felt, and a feeling of awe made all his limbs tremble and shake.

At first he thought the puppets were working, so purposefully and steadily did they circulate, their heads bent low, their shoulders crouched, their bodies moving with a dragging motion as if they drew some invisible force behind them. Although they did not hold hands it seemed as if some united effort joined every puppet to his neighbour, and through this swaying, hauling mass of wooden people someone was now pushing his way like a dark shadow among all the gay dresses.

Thrusting the puppets to right and to left a figure advanced that Rudi recognized from long years past as Malkin, the wicked toymaker of Pils, whom the King had once banished from his kingdom, and who was trying now to ruin the people of Drüssl and win the whole Mountain for his own.

'Good day, Rudi Toymaker!' he greeted him in a mocking voice. 'I hear an accident has befallen you! Young men are not always prudent when they climb in the mountains! I hope you have no serious injury?'

'I am sorry to disappoint you if you wished to break my neck, Malkin Toymaker!' Rudi said scornfully. 'But fortunately I am not the only strong man left in Drüssl! Our pile of tree trunks grows bigger every day behind the burgomaster's house, and I do not think you have advanced much in magic since you left the kingdom, Master Malkin, if you have not found a way to outwit us long before this!'

Malkin's face grew red with anger but he kept his temper and spoke with a silky tongue.

'You may be interested to judge my magic for yourself, friend Rudi!' he said. 'Come with me and I will show you what all these wooden people are doing!'

He led Rudi through the moving crowds to a small door behind one of the pillars in the hall. The door was studded with diamonds and rubies. It was guarded by two sentries.

When the sentries saw Malkin they immediately presented arms, at the same time giving him a look of hatred and contempt. Malkin merely pressed four fingertips on the panel above the door, and it opened quietly.

Inside was another door, also guarded by sentries, and then a third and a fourth. Each door was covered with precious stones and guarded by puppet soldiers. The last door was the most splendid of all, and it was guarded by two puppets who bore a remarkable likeness to the soldier dolls once belonging to Paul and Peterkin.

Rudi hardly gave them a second glance for Malkin was murmuring words he could not catch as he stood facing the door, and at once it opened to let them pass inside. As they stepped over the threshold it closed with a clang behind them.

Inside the room was a sight Rudi would never never forget, though he lived to be a hundred years old, or older than old Peter Toymaker. Suspended in space it seemed, was the Mountain's heart, throbbing like a splendid jewel. The beat of it echoed steadily throughout the rocky vault, vibrating from the walls: Tick-*tock*! Tick-*tock*! Tick-*tock*!

'Here is a sight few have ever seen, and a sound that

few have heard!' said Malkin proudly. 'Do you hear it, Rudi Toymaker? Tick-*tock*! Tick-*tock*! Tick-*tock*! Once, not so very long ago it beat *Tick*-tock! *Tick*-tock! *Tick*-tock! But I have altered all that! I am moving the Mountain – I, Malkin Toymaker who was humiliated and chased from the kingdom and banished! *I* am doing this thing! You saw the wooden people in the hall there? They move round and round as I tell them to do, drawing the Mountain in the right direction. They will not stop while the heart is beating and the heart will not stop beating while they move. But it is not the puppet people who have changed the beat of the Mountain's heart! It is I alone, Malkin the Toymaker, with my magic key!'

Rudi could see a tiny keyhole in the apex of the great beating heart. Malkin watched him keenly.

'The key is destroyed!' he cried triumphantly. 'Gone for ever! I melted it in the hottest fires my blacksmiths could kindle! It will never fit the keyhole again. Never, never!'

Strong man as he was, Rudi shuddered at the awful fate of the Mountain. Then he met Malkin's gaze with a look so bold and scornful that it was Malkin's turn to quail

'Out of here!' he commanded, and Rudi walked back through the series of doors into the hall.

The wooden puppets were endlessly toiling, but they had moved towards the walls to make way for a beautiful girl who was approaching. Rudi would have sworn her person was not made of flesh and blood, yet her skin was so pink and white and satiny it hardly looked like wood or china.

The puppets bowed or curtseyed when she passed

them. They did not appear only to respect her, it was more like adoration. She murmured a kind word to this one or that as she approached Malkin and Rudi, holding both little white hands outstretched, her face uplifted in sympathy and kindness. Her head came no higher than Rudi's waist.

'Poor, poor Rudi!' said this beautiful girl, the first pleasant sound he had heard since his fall into the chasm. 'What have they done to you?'

Then turning on Malkin her black eyes flashed anger and scorn as she upbraided him.

'Wicked Malkin! How can you treat an honest man so? Is your own art fallen so low that you must always cheat to win? Send the soldiers away and let Rudi Toymaker go free!'

Malkin glowered at her, but without waiting she clapped her hands and cried: 'Guards! Dismiss!' The soldiers fell out at once, rapidly disappearing among the crowd of workers.

Bewildered, Rudi stared first at the girl and then at the toymaker. Was this Queen that the puppets worshipped and obeyed really Malkin's doll of long ago? He remembered her as a pretty toy in an embroidered dress, a very different being from this gracious lady with her voice so full of compassion, her eyes warm with sympathy and pity. Yet there was something familiar about her, something young and ageless . . .

'Poor Rudi!' the Queen said. 'We will not keep you prisoner here. You must go back to your Margaret and your babies at home. But first we must bind up your wounds or your wife will be worried to see you with blood upon your face.'

She led him into a sort of ante-room, where two wooden puppets brought warm water and soft cloths with which she wiped Rudi's bruises and bound up his cuts. As her white hands gently washed his face he was aware that they were by no means made of real flesh and blood. They were neither warm nor soft, but cold and hard, like hands made from some artificial material. At once he became alert, sensing danger, for hands like these could only be the handiwork of Malkin the wicked Toymaker of Pils.

He pretended to be grateful however, and bowed low, thanking her when she had finished.

'And now gracious Queen,' he added, 'I beg you to show me the way out of this Mountain, because I fell from a very great height, and the walls of the chasm are so steep and slippery that with my broken axe I should never be able to climb them again!'

A sly look crept into the eyes of the doll-Queen.

'Just a little patience, Rudi!' she told him. 'You shall go home – but not today! Only a little while longer and Malkin will have moved the whole Mountain over the borders into his own country. Then the people of Drüssl will lose their trades and starve, but *you* shall fetch your wife and children to come and live here, yes! and your young brother too, and old Peter Toymaker if you want them with you. When you make your home in this country Malkin means to appoint you his Master Toymaker! Think how rich you will become! All your children will be princes! Only a few more days and everything will turn out for the best!'

Rudi sprang to his feet in a rage.

'I will *never* work for Malkin Toymaker!' he shouted.

'Poor Malkin! Nobody says a good word for him!' the
Queen said pensively. 'But the people here love me, and
I love my people. Once the Mountain is ours we will get
rid of Malkin by some means or another and when I am
Queen all alone I can do as I please. Your family shall
have the highest position in the land, Rudi Toymaker,
and every pine tree on the Mountain shall be your own
property.'

But Rudi sank his head into his hands with a groan of
misery. When he looked up the Queen was gone and the
door guarded by a dozen sentries. There seemed to be no
other entrance to the room.

Rudi was now positive that the Queen was Malkin's

doll Marta, who in just failing to win the King's prize had disgraced herself and her master and been banished from the kingdom for ever. She had not grown much taller, and her womanliness was no more convincing than her innocence had been in days gone by. When she did not return and no one else came near him he threw himself on a couch at the side of the ante-room and presently fell asleep from sheer exhaustion.

Life became a kind of dream for Rudi.

He was given handsome rooms to live in, delicious food, and fine clothes to wear. He ate some of the food, but refused to wear the clothes that were so different from his homespuns, woven by Margaret.

The Queen was always kind and gracious to him even when he ignored her. She liked to sit beside him at her embroidery frame or her painting. She was painting a portrait of his head.

Rudi was not entirely a prisoner, in that he was allowed to come and go in the hall, by order of the doll-Queen. He was even permitted to visit the Mountain's heart, but wherever he went she followed him.

He studied the heart very carefully, but with little hope that he could ever defeat the magic of the wicked toymaker.

Malkin was often to be found in the inner room, gloating over the progress of his work. If he met him there Rudi walked straight out again. There was nothing he wished to say to Malkin and no hope of mercy from him.

Beyond the hall he could not go. Every entrance was manned by wooden soldiers and he was watched and guarded wherever he went.

8

THE FINDING OF RUDI

At home, Anders found himself forced to take Rudi's place as the head of the family.

Old Peter Toymaker was failing, stricken with grief at Rudi's disappearance. The twins were very young. Elizabeth could not understand why her father never came home. Margaret relied on her young brother-in-law for comfort and help, and Anders did all he could to console and support her.

But he begged her not to prevent him and the twins from searching the Mountain every day. 'For these are Rudi's sons,' he told her gravely. 'And I am his brother. Who else is going to save him if we do not?'

He told Margaret that twins are protected against magic powers if they walk hand in hand, which comforted their mother so greatly that she bound their little fingers together with scarlet thread in case they forgot. She insisted that they should come home at meal times, although Anders might return at what hours he chose. But to reassure her he carried Rudi's new horn slung round his neck blowing it once in every hour to show Margaret that he was still safe and unharmed. The echoes of the horn rolled joyfully down to Drüssl, putting new heart into the anxious village. Anders felt very important.

The twins felt important too, since none of the other children in Drüssl were allowed by their mothers to cross the bed of the stream. When meal times came Paul and Peterkin paraded home hand in hand along the village street, dragging great boughs of green pine that they had gathered on the Mountain. Together they searched every crack and cranny they could find, hoping

that it might lead to some deep gorge or chasm where Rudi might be hidden.

They were helped by the trolls and goblins living on the lower slopes. These were too frightened of the little wooden soldiers and their cannons to venture higher, but they kept an eye on the Mountain's movement and reported its progress. They had not seen Rudi fall, but like Anders and the twins, they felt certain he was not dead, but hidden away somewhere, unable to find his way home.

One day Paul and Peterkin met one of the mountain trolls near the old stepping stones where once the tumbling stream had flowed.

'A new crack has appeared along this bank!' the troll said excitedly. 'It is very deep and runs far inside the Mountain! We dared not go inside it for fear of what the puppet people might do to us!'

In a moment the twins were poking their faces into the bracken, where they discovered a deep crack gashing the lowest slopes of the Mountain, just as the troll had described. Paul was the first to scramble into the fissure with Peterkin pressing on his heels. The crack widened into a passage, smelling sweetly of new earth and the roots of growing things. It led them further than any crack had led them yet. The daylight faded slowly behind them.

Paul began to flag. Peterkin, who could still see the sunlight like a friendly star in their wake, urged him to go on.

'It's so dark!' Paul whimpered. 'You lead, Peterkin!'

Over his brother's shoulder Peterkin could see the passage like a dark cave ahead, leading on to deeper darkness, and he too hesitated.

'Perhaps we ought to fetch Uncle Anders!' he said.

They hurried back to the entrance where the troll was still waiting for them. Obligingly he hurried off to fetch Anders, whose horn could be heard only a short distance above them among the trees. They heard him describing to the troll how all the tree stumps had now moved over the summit into Malkin's country and the wicked toy-maker was fast capturing the pine trees themselves.

Anders jumped into the crack and led the twins down the dark passage which did not seem nearly so terrifying when they were walking behind his broad and familiar back.

The daylight faded away behind them and the anxious inquiries of their friend the Mountain troll, could no longer be heard. Out of the earth and the deepness of the Mountain came a pale, mysterious fairy light to help them on their way. All three holding fast to one another they could see the passage winding on and on ahead of them as they pressed one upon another's heels.

How far they had gone none of them could tell, when suddenly Anders announced: 'It is getting narrower – much narrower now!' A little later he said: 'I can see the passage is coming to an end, just like all the other cracks did. It isn't any better than the rest after all!'

The twins were so disappointed they were ready to burst into tears, and a few feet further on Anders came to a sudden stop, so unexpectedly that Paul and Peterkin bruised their noses by bumping into one another's backs.

'I can't go any farther!' Anders said. 'It is so narrow now my shoulders are rubbing the sides and my head touches the roof. I can't quite see the end but we must be nearly there. We shall have to go home.'

Their feet stopped scraping and shuffling, and for one moment all three stood in the deep silence of the Mountain, preparing to turn round. But in that moment a faraway muffled noise met their ears, an irregular sound like a throb, far beyond them, drowned in earth and rock and darkness, yet active and real and alive . . .

Tick-*tock*! Tick-*tock*! Tick-*tock*!

'It sounds like Uncle Peter's heart when we sit on his knees!' said Peterkin, wondering.

'Or Mitzi cat when I press my head into her side!' said Paul.

'It *is* a heart!' said Anders, excitedly. 'It is the heart of the Mountain that we can hear!'

The twins felt their own hearts leap at this announcement. Never had they imagined being so close to such a mysterious thing.

'Can't we go on and see?' Paul said, half hopeful, half frightened.

'But I'm too big to get any farther,' Anders said. 'You two might be able to. Would you like to try?'

The twins agreed, shivering with anticipation and terror. All three retreated down the passage till it was wide enough for Paul and Peterkin to pass Anders and walk ahead.

'Which of you is going first?' Anders asked them.

'I am!' said Paul.

'No, I am!' said Peterkin.

'I'm the elder!' Paul said.

'But I'm thinner than you!' said Peterkin.

So he led, with Paul close behind him and Anders holding on to Paul's belt, in the rear.

At last the passage became so narrow that he had to let go. 'I can't follow you now. I shall stick fast if I do!' he said. 'But nothing can hurt you while you are together. I will wait for you here.'

The twins went bravely forward, hand in hand, and found that the passage was just wide enough for them to wriggle through. In a little while it stopped getting narrower and wound its way on towards the throbbing sound that grew louder and louder.

'Are you frightened, Peterkin?' Paul whispered.

'Yes I am a little!' Peterkin confessed. 'Can you still see Uncle Anders?'

'No, we have turned too many corners, but I heard him whistle to us just now.'

'Let's call to him!' said Peterkin. They called, and along the corridor came the faint reassuring message of Anders' horn. Greatly heartened the twins pressed on again.

Tick-*tock*! Tick-*tock*! Now the throbbing seemed to thunder down the passage, shaking the very walls. They must be getting very close to the heart of the Mountain. But again the tunnel was dwindling at every step. The ceiling sloped so steeply downwards that, small as they were, they were forced to stoop. For several yards they tunnelled their way on with great courage, and then Peterkin cried out sharply: 'Oh! oh! we can't go any further now! It has come to an end!'

'*Push!*' cried Paul impatiently, above the enormous booming of the heart that seemed to be all about their ears. They were so close to it now that they could not bear to be thwarted, but although they pushed and shoved and kicked, and hammered with their boots the wall of earth before them did not give way, although it seemed that it was not really very solid. A hollow sound met their frantic blows, while beyond it just on the other

side, perhaps! The great heart was beating, beating, beating . . .

Their excitement was so intense that they had lost all fear of the heartbeats but inched and scraped by turns, going back every short while to a spot where the tunnel was wide enough for them to change places so that the other could do his share of burrowing.

All of a sudden, Peterkin cried. 'My hand has gone through! There is a hollow space beyond and I can put my arm in it!'

By shovelling and scraping he made the space large enough to put his head inside the hollow darkness, where he announced that he could see a little light – just a very little point like a star, shining in one corner.

'Whatever can it be?' wondered Paul. 'Let's make the hole bigger then perhaps we can creep through it and see the heart of the Mountain!'

But they had scraped all the loose earth away. The hole was edged with rock, and it was with the greatest difficulty that the two little boys at last thrust their bodies through and found themselves inside a cupboard, built into the face of the rock. The small point of light they had seen was in fact a crack in a door, while on the other side the tremendous thundering of the Mountain's heart drowned anything that they might say to one another, until Paul, putting his eye to the chink let out such a cry of joy that the tunnel rang with it even above the heart-beats – for the chink presented to him the interior of a brilliantly lit chamber hung with silken hangings and furnished with embroidered chairs and couches. There, in front of a glowing fire, sitting with his head bowed in his hands as if all hope had left him, sat Rudi, their father!

'It's Father!' shouted Peterkin joyfully.

'Father!' echoed Paul.

Rudi started from his chair, looking wildly round. For once he had been left alone, since escape was impossible. The doll-Queen had gone to prepare a special supper for him with her own hands.

'Father!' the twins shouted together at the tops of their voices.

Rudi sprang to the door and opened it. When he saw the happy dirty faces of his little boys inside the cupboard, tears of joy filled his own eyes, followed by an expression of great anxiety.

'How did you come here?' he asked as he hugged them, afraid that they too had fallen down a chasm in the mountainside.

'By a long, long passage that leads from the stream!'
the twins reassured him. 'Uncle Anders came along as
far as he could and then we came alone. Come back with
us quickly, Father! we have all missed you so badly and
nobody cuts down any pine trees now! But first will you
show us the heart of the Mountain that is beating so
loudly so close to us? and then will you help us to make
the hole a little bigger so that you can come back to
Mother with us and show Uncle Anders you are safe?'

'No! No! You must not come in here!' Rudi said
hastily. 'I will come back with you if I can. But first of all
tell me how far the Mountain has moved since I went
away?'

'Oh I don't know how far it has moved since then!'
Paul said. 'But last week I heard the burgomaster saying
to John Carpenter that in another week it would be over
the border at the rate it is travelling now.'

Rudi gave a groan. 'I must come quickly if anything is
to be done!' he said. 'Back through the hole both of you,
directly, for I am coming too!'

But the hole was much too small for Rudi's great
shoulders, and if the passage beyond was too narrow for
Anders how could Rudi hope to get himself through it?
The solid rock would not yield. He would never get out
that way.

The twins burst into tears of despair.

'Hush! Be brave and patient!' Rudi said. 'Go back
and tell your mother that I am safe and well, but that
Malkin and his doll-Queen keep me prisoner here. I will
come back to her as soon as I can. Come and see me from
time to time and tell me what is happening to the Mountain, but be very careful and quiet. You must *never* be

discovered here so be careful to look through the chink first and find out if I am alone! Hush! Somebody is coming!'

He closed the cupboard door. Peeping through the chink the twins now saw a beautiful lady come into the room. She wore a gown of crimson and gold and carried a silver tray covered with dishes and delicious food, and a bowl of fruit.

'Isn't she beautiful?' Paul whispered to Peterkin, 'and she seems to be very kind to poor Father!'

Full of excitement they crept along the passage to tell their story to Anders, who was just as excited as themselves to know Rudi's hiding place was discovered, but he shook his head over the description of the beautiful lady.

'Not a Queen but a wicked doll!' he told them. 'Malkin made her many years ago. She is false and not to be trusted. I think you had better not talk about anything you have seen when you get back to the village. Tell nobody except your mother that your father is found. It is going to be very difficult and dangerous to rescue him, and the fewer people who know about it, the less likely it is that the news will reach Malkin's ears.'

It was not easy for Paul and Peterkin to keep their secret when they reached home, but once Elizabeth and the baby were put to bed they climbed on to their mother's knees and gave her the wonderful news she had waited for during so many long and dreary days. Rudi was safe, but a prisoner locked inside the mountain. Old Peter Toymaker too was let into the secret and the years seemed to roll off his shoulders as he heard it.

But after the first joy came the question: how was Rudi to be rescued?

Anders did not share with his family the dreadful news that one of the trolls had told him – how, if Malkin succeeded in moving the whole of the Mountain over the border into Malkin's country, everything upon it would immediately fall into Malkin's power and either turn into stone, be crumbled into dust, or become subject entirely to the toymaker's will. He could not bear to damp Margaret's joy just when her heart was full of hope.

'We must keep in close touch with Rudi!' he told her and the twins. 'Sooner or later we shall find a way to rescue him, and meanwhile either you, Paul, or you, Peterkin, must keep constant guard inside the cupboard and find out what is going on.'

He thought of asking the mountain trolls and goblins to widen the hole with their picks and shovels but if the faintest clink were heard inside the room where Rudi was imprisoned all hope of rescue would be over.

So the next day all three returned to the crack in the Mountain, the twins carrying a couple of Rudi's favourite cookies that their mother had baked for him, wrapped in a clean white handkerchief.

'Why are you so happy again Mother?' little Elizabeth asked when the boys had gone. 'Is Father soon coming home?'

'I hope so! oh I hope so!' Margaret said, but she was careful not to display her new happiness in front of the neighbours.

Meanwhile the twins retraced their footsteps along the passage, but they had to wait for a long while inside the cupboard until Rudi was alone. When at last all his attendants had left him they called him as gently as they could above the heart-beats, and Rudi came at once to the cupboard door.

'Brave fellows!' he exclaimed, eagerly biting into one of Margaret's cakes. 'Oh how these cookies make me think of home! How is dear old Uncle Peter? and my sweet Elizabeth? and that young scamp your baby brother? Do you obey your mother always, and help her, and do as Anders tells you, my brave boys?'

The twins were pouring out news of home and village when all of a sudden Rudi sprang away from the door. Someone was coming into the ante-chamber behind him.

'Dear Rudi! Malkin the Toymaker wishes to see you in the hall of the heart of the Mountain!' the doll-Queen said, in a voice that was at the same time soothing and sly. 'He has important news to tell you!'

The twins watched their father leave the room behind the beautiful lady.

For a long time they waited for his return, but when he came back he was alone. He sat down with his head in his hands and an expression of such despair on his face that Paul and Peterkin did not like to question him.

'Six days longer!' he said aloud at last. 'And then the Mountain will be Malkin's and I shall be his slave.' There followed another despairing silence before Rudi sprang to his feet.

'I *must* save the Mountain!' he exclaimed. 'I *must* save the Mountain!' And all of a sudden a new light broke out on his face. He bounded over to the cupboard and put his face close against the faces of his sons.

'Listen carefully to what I tell you!' he ordered them. 'Every word is important and you must remember everything I say! Malkin has destroyed the key of the Mountain. The key was made of pure gold and I must have a new one. There is no gold left inside the Mountain, for Malkin knows that gold is pure and true and will thwart his magic powers. A new key must be made to fit the Mountain's heart and to change the beat of it, and only I who have seen the keyhole, can make such a key. Tell Anders to bring me enough gold to make a key that is as long as my little finger and as slim as the twig of a birch tree. Tell him too to bring me my tools, but you must not say anything to anybody outside our home. News travels quicker underground than through the air, and I am constantly afraid that Malkin's people will discover the passage. Remember everything that I have told you!'

The twins went back to tell their news to Anders. With their spirits soaring they returned home and told Margaret and old Peter Toymaker. The whole family now believed that without any shadow of doubt not only Rudi, but the whole of their beloved Mountain would be saved.

9

SEARCHING FOR GOLD

And now began the search for gold.

Margaret at once slipped the wedding ring off her finger. 'This will make a start!' she said.

But the little family, though respectable and well provided for, was not wealthy – Rudi and Margaret were too generous to hoard up riches, and their savings were in silver only. Though they searched the house from top to bottom they could not find a single gold piece.

They looked at each other in distress.

'Could the goblins help us?' Margaret asked Anders, but he shook his head. 'Goblin gold is of no use to us,' he said. 'It will not make Rudi's key. We shall have to borrow from the burgomaster.'

Old Peter Toymaker agreed. 'This is no time for pride, nor for prattling,' he said, 'we must certainly ask the burgomaster to help us. But he must not know what we want the money for.'

Margaret went at once to the burgomaster's house, and although her cheeks flushed scarlet and she plucked nervously at her apron with her hands, she asked him bravely to lend them a piece of gold.

The burgomaster was only too willing to oblige her. He was too considerate to ask questions, but he felt deeply concerned to think that Rudi's family was in want. The moment Margaret had gone he rushed to his wife and told her to have the fattest rooster killed and plucked and dressed and sent as a present to the Toymaker's family, who must be very sorely pressed since his disappearance if his wife had come asking for the loan of a piece of gold. He felt quite depressed about it.

Margaret would have been overcome with shame at accepting such a present, if it had not arrived at the most opportune moment possible. For while she had been at the burgomaster's house a coach had driven up and deposited at her door none other than her beloved friend and sister-in-law, Elsa, Rudi's only sister, who was court dressmaker in the city below, and whose rare visits were always an occasion of feasting and rejoicing.

So the burgomaster's chicken was cooked and eaten very gratefully, between welcoming Elsa and mourning at the news they had to tell her.

At last the younger children were tucked up in bed and the two women sat round the fire to talk, while Elsa did the fine repairs on little garments at which she excelled, and Margaret poured out their story, ending with the problem that was now ahead – how to obtain enough pure gold to make a new key, so that Rudi could save himself and the Mountain before Malkin engulfed them both.

'And I left my earrings and my gold chain at home!' cried Elsa, in an agony of self-reproach. 'I thought it would be silly to wear them travelling through the forest, for fear of meeting robbers and thieves. But I have my gold scissors with me!'

Old Peter Toymaker was weighing Margaret's wedding ring and the burgomaster's gold piece in the palm of his hand.

'Not so very much is lacking!' he said thoughtfully. 'The weight of the scissors might be just enough!'

But when Elsa began to hunt for her scissors they were not to be found. She looked in her needlecase, in the bag that held her bobbins, in her pocket, and even in her sleeves. The whole family turned the kitchen upside down without a trace of the missing scissors.

'I know I unpacked them, for I cut out a paper doll for Elizabeth, before she went to bed!' Elsa said, but as she spoke a commotion could be heard upstairs. They could hear scolding and sobbing and the patter of bare feet, as down the stairs came little Elizabeth, escorted by her angry brothers, Paul holding her by one arm and Peterkin by the other. Tears were streaming down her face.

In the folds of her long white nightdress she was hiding something that her brothers were trying to take away.

'Look at this naughty girl!' said Paul.

'You don't know what she has done!' said Peterkin.

'She has stolen Aunt Elsa's scissors!' cried Paul.

'And cut off all her hair!' shouted Peterkin.

'Just look at her now!' they said in chorus, pushing Elizabeth into the circle beside the fire.

Elizabeth broke away from them and flew into her mother's arms. The scissors fell to the floor. A shower of golden curls fell with them and her shocked family saw that her head was shorn of everything but a mass of short

curls that clustered in ragged confusion around her ears.

'I wanted gold for Father!' Elizabeth sobbed with her face buried in her mother's neck.

'Isn't she a *silly*!' Paul and Peterkin said in disgust.

It appeared that she had heard her brothers talking in bed upstairs when they thought she was asleep. They were planning how to get enough gold for their father to make the precious key that would rescue him.

'What is gold?' she asked them.

'Go to sleep! Gold is yellow stuff! Your hair is gold!' the twins had told her. So Elizabeth had taken out Aunt Elsa's scissors that she had not been able to resist taking up to bed with her, and had cut off all her golden hair 'for Father'.

'She's so *silly*!' the twins repeated.

Anders burst out laughing. Margaret comforted her sobbing daughter while old Peter Toymaker picked up the scissors and a handful of curls.

'Who knows if we may not have enough gold here, after all?' he said, weighing them thoughtfully. 'You should be ashamed to scoff at your little sister, Paul and Peterkin, for who knows what magic may lie in the gift of a loving heart? Elizabeth is as anxious to serve her father as you are.'

The twins now felt ashamed of themselves and begged Elizabeth's pardon. They swept up the rest of the curls very carefully and stored them away with the gold coin, the scissors and Margaret's wedding ring in the bag they now used to carry their dinner in, since their work had become too important for them to come home for meals.

All three went off to bed, where their elders soon followed them, all anxious for the next day to come, so that the gold could be put into Rudi's hands and he might begin to put into force the work that must be finished before the next five days had passed.

10

THE PUPPET PRINCE

Paul and Peterkin were awake at daybreak. They scrambled into their clothes and were off to the Mountain, hardly waiting to drink their mugs of milk or eat the rolls that Margaret had buttered for them.

Anders heard them going and hurried after them. He did not want them to go far out of his sight, but by the time he reached the crack in the stream bank they were already far down the tunnel and could be neither seen nor heard.

Anders thought the Mountain seemed unusually restless. Every few minutes the earth seemed to shake and quiver, while the pine trees moaned and sighed in the windless air. Everywhere was uneasiness and unrest.

'Things must be reaching a climax!' Anders said to himself. 'Malkin said the end would come in six days. I would not expect it to last as long as that.'

A troll popped out of the tunnel's entrance to tell him that the twins were safely past.

'But things are getting worse!' he added piteously, 'the wooden soldiers grow more daring every day. They throw stones at us and fire cannon-balls down the Mountain with their wooden cannons. Most of us trolls and goblins have left the Mountain. Only those of us who have treasure buried here stay. We dig it at night

when Malkin's people cannot see us. But they have
guessed what we are doing, and already they are cross-
ing the border to try to steal it. Soon we shall have to
leave it behind or Malkin will make us all his prisoners
and what can we do then?'

'It is true that we have not much longer,' Anders said.
'But don't lose heart, and try to prevent the rest of your
friends from leaving the Mountain. We may need their
help. Don't talk about it, but it is still possible that the
Mountain may be saved!'

The troll stared at him in disbelief.

'We used to say that Rudi would save us,' he said. 'But
the weeks and days went by and where is Rudi now?
Nobody talks about him any more, but we are taking
away our treasure to hide it in safer places.'

'Never lose hope!' Anders said stubbornly. Leaving
the little man still staring he followed the twins inside the
Mountain.

He had not gone far before he found them coming
back in high spirits.

'Uncle Anders! Father has the gold safely! He says he
has enough to make the golden key. But he says he
cannot make it while the doll-Queen watches him night
and day and tells all that he does to Malkin. He says it
will take hours to make the key and she never leaves him
alone. Father wants you to make him something to distract her attention – another doll, a little prince, he says,
and you are to use his best wood and best tools and ask
Uncle Peter how you are to do it. And when Father
heard Aunt Elsa had come to visit us he said she could
dress the doll as nobody else in the world could do it.
Let's get back quickly so we can begin at once!'

Anders hurried home quite shattered by the responsibility of undertaking such a task. He had never attempted to make anything so ambitious. But the need was so urgent that there was no question of refusing, and he told the family as briefly as he could the plan that was in Rudi's mind. The cottage at once became a hive of activity.

'There is a fine piece of wood behind the door in the shed,' Anders said, going to fetch it, while Elsa sorted out the scraps of silk and satin she had brought up from the city for the dressing of Elizabeth's dolls.

'We must keep the children in the house!' Margaret said anxiously. 'Elizabeth may prattle, while Paul and Peterkin are so bursting with self-importance that anyone could guess they have something to hide. Once the secret is out it will spread like wildfire round the village and may reach Malkin's ears.'

'Nobody must come into the house either,' old Peter Toymaker said. 'Otherwise they will want to know what we are doing, and every moment is precious now. You must send all the neighbours away, Margaret.'

So Margaret told the neighbours that the children had an infectious fever, when they came knocking on the door. She felt ashamed at deceiving them, for she was an honest girl, but the children enjoyed the game, rushing upstairs when anyone came, and stifling their giggles in the counterpane. Once the neighbour retreated the twins and Elizabeth came down again to watch Anders carving his puppet prince under the guidance of old Peter Toymaker, whose fingers were now too stiff to hold a knife. Elsa sat stitching beside them, making a velvet cap and doublet worthy of a wooden prince.

Their work was carried out with anxious hearts and in great fear. They all knew the time and care Rudi would put into such an enterprise, how he would spend days and weeks in making the features lifelike, the limbs flexible and natural, the proportions normal, but further than twenty-four hours they dared not wait, so they worked doggedly on, ignoring the food that Margaret put before them, and presently even their conversation died away.

The day seemed longest for Margaret, who could only wait, clear away the uneaten food, amuse the restless children and wonder whether she would ever see her husband again.

Bedtime came at last for the children, but the older people worked on far into the night, carving, polishing, painting, stitching, till long after the moon had set the puppet prince stood at last upon its feet, dressed in the finest clothes Elsa could contrive for it, and gazing around with a foolish simper that was the best that Anders' inexperience could do with its face.

Speech he was not able to give it, but a few tricks learnt from hanging about Malkin's workshop as a small boy had endowed it with some movement and at least the appearance of being alive.

To Elizabeth's great surprise, when she ran downstairs in the morning and attempted to take the puppet in her arms, it sprang to its feet, bowed, and gently kissed her hand.

The twins could not believe their eyes.

'How shall we get it to the Mountain without everybody in the village seeing it?' they asked.

'I have got idea!' said Anders. 'One of you twins

must go first to the Mountain taking this wooden fellow with you, dressed in some of your clothes. We can tie its little finger to yours, just as people always see you walking hand in hand. Some time later the other twin must go out alone to join them. Nobody knows which is Paul

and which is Peterkin. They will simply think one of you has come back to fetch something and is starting out again.'

'That is a wonderful idea!' said Paul. 'I shall go first, with the doll.'

'No, I shall!' said Peterkin.

'If you quarrel about it then I shall go myself, with the puppet prince dressed up in your clothes!' Anders threatened them, so for the sake of peace they agreed to draw lots and Paul drew the longest straw.

Anders covered up the doll prince's fine clothes with a jacket and trousers belonging to the twins, and tied its little finger to Paul's. It felt hard and scratchy, Paul said, after his brother's hand.

Everything fell out just as Anders had planned. The village people were so used to seeing the twins set off together for the Mountain that nobody stopped them or looked too closely under the prince's old felt hat.

One neighbour called out to ask if they were all better this morning, and Paul answered cheerfully that their fever had gone in the night.

Half an hour later Peterkin dodged round the back of the houses and joined his twin brother at the tunnel's entrance. Anders was not long behind them. He unfastened the puppet prince and tied the twins' fingers together again.

'Listen to me!' he told them. 'I think it would be very unwise to take this puppet up the tunnel to Rudi's prison. Everyone will want to know how he arrived, and the guards may look into the cupboard and discover the passage, which would be very dangerous indeed. The only way to send him into Malkin's kingdom is by the chasm where Rudi fell. We can throw the doll down after him.'

'But supposing he breaks?' said the twins.

'Wooden puppets don't break as easily as that!' said Anders. 'And our Rudi landed quite safely after all! Follow me! We must find the chasm as quickly as we can!'

Rudi had described to the twins as nearly as possible

the place where he fell, but Anders was afraid the chasm might have moved by now into Malkin's country. He did not want the twins to run any risk, so left them searching the lower slopes with the puppet prince while he climbed the Mountain to see what he could discover.

The wooden soldiers were everywhere above him. Anders could hear the click of their arms and see glimpses of their uniforms among the pine trees. He dodged from trunk to trunk keeping out of view and watching them.

At the place Rudi had described to the twins the undergrowth was very thick. Anders went down on his hands and knees, worming his way along until suddenly his knee slipped into a crack half filled with brambles.

Pushing them away he saw it was the very end of a long fissure that ran uphill to a line of rocks and disappeared beneath them, growing wilder and deeper all the time. Anders could see that by the time it reached the rocks the fissure was very deep indeed.

His heart bounded with hope.

Where the crack plunged into the ground there were very few soldiers, although Anders could see a kind of camp not far away, with a stew pot and a couple of guards sitting beside it polishing their cannons with handfuls of dry pine needles.

Very cautiously he crept upwards from rock to pine trunk and from pine trunk to rock, until he was right underneath the line of rocks and realized he had arrived at the boundary of Malkin's land.

The crack seemed to plunge underneath the line of rocks and continue on the other side. Finding a space

between two stones Anders put his eye to it and saw two
sentries standing just beyond him on the brink of the
chasm, tossing pebbles into the deeps.

'One – two – three! I heard it hit the bottom!' he
heard one of them say. 'It must be twenty feet deep if it is
an inch!'

'A little higher up and you can count seven before it
strikes!' the other said, 'better not drop your musket
down or you'll never see it again!'

'And not fifty yards above our heads you cannot hear
a stone hit the bottom at all!' the first soldier said. 'But if
you lie down and listen, you can hear the Mountain's
heart beating down there far below us. Tick-*tock*! tick-
tock! tick-*tock*! I wonder how much longer it will go
on!'

At that moment a terrible tremor shook the earth.
Anders, springing back was just in time to save his toes
from being crushed as the whole line of rocks on the
boundary lurched forwards and upwards, letting fall a
shower of fragments in its wake.

The soldiers ran to move their camping place and
cooking pots into safety. Anders took advantage of their
confusion to run back into cover of the trees, and he ran
downhill to tell the twins what he had heard and seen.

He found them telling stories to the puppet prince
who showed no interest whatever.

'I have found the crack!' Anders told them. 'But it is
so guarded by Malkin's men in its deepest part that I
cannot see how we are going to drop our prince inside it.
I wish we could get something to distract their attention,
but what could it be?'

'They like music!' Paul announced with assurance.

'And dancing!' Peterkin added.

'And singing!' said Paul.

'And all kinds of shouting and hopping about!' finished Peterkin.

Anders looked at the pair of them in amazement.

'How do you know all this?' he asked them.

'Oh, we often go and talk to them!' the twins explained. 'Before we discovered the tunnel we were always up there on the boundary. They used to help us to look for Father. They were sorry for us, they said.'

'But didn't they shoot at you?' asked Anders, astonished at their story.

'Oh no! Mother tied our fingers together you know! And besides, we used to amuse them and make them laugh. We used to sing and dance for them till they cracked their sides. You ought to have seen them, Uncle Anders!'

'And you never breathed a word about it!' reproved Anders, eyeing his astonishing nephews severely.

'Well, no. You see, Mother is so particular about that kind of thing!' said the twins, wriggling about in their shoes. 'And of course, once Father was found we never went back to see them any more, but I am sure they will be very glad to see us again!'

'You mustn't tell them that we have found your father,' Anders warned them. 'If they ask you, say you have no idea when he will come home again. They have wooden heads, so that will satisfy them for the present. All right then! Run along and find them, and if you can keep them entertained and hold their attention for ten minutes or so I will take the prince with me and drop him into the chasm.'

Paul and Peterkin scampered off in the direction of the boundary while Anders led the puppet prince uphill keeping as far as possible out of sight.

Before climbing over the boundary he went to some trouble to find out what the twins were up to, and whether they could really hold the attention of the wooden soldiers long enough for him to carry out his mission.

Roars of flat laughter and the clapping of wooden hands told him that the twins had at least been welcomed. Presently he caught sight of them in a little glade some distance above, capering and dancing and performing all kinds of ridiculous antics of a kind that always sent Elizabeth and their baby brother into fits of laughter, but which usually annoyed and irritated the grown-ups very much indeed.

Anders laughed to himself as he watched their wildly waving arms and legs and heard their shrill voices chanting some graceless ditty. The soldiers were enjoying themselves. Dozens of little wooden heads popped over the rocks to watch the twins, and slowly the circle around them became more and more crowded, until the part of the boundary striding the chasm was completely deserted.

Anders scrambled across the rocks dragging the puppet prince behind him, tearing his clothes and barking his shins in an attempt to protect the wooden doll's satin tunic and cloak, which had not been made for such rough handling.

He was over the top at last. The soldiers were still watching the twins when Anders stopped behind a pine tree, creeping step by step along the brink of the ever deepening chasm.

It was just as the sentry had described it. Fifty yards from the boundary rocks the crack plunged down into such frightful depth and darkness that anyone might have thought it bottomless.

Anders stared with horror into its gloomy void. How could Rudi possibly have escaped with his life, falling into such a terrible place? Was he really alive, somewhere down there below him? Anders lay flat on his face to listen.

Above his head, a little wind sighed in the pine trees. The wooden soldiers laughed and clapped. The twins sang their shrill choruses, but above all these sounds, yet far, far below him Anders could hear the sound that the sentry had described. Tick-*tock*! Tick-*tock*! Tick-*tock*! It was the heart of the Mountain beating.

If Rudi was really alive in those depths there was no time to be lost. The puppet prince must go after him, and holding him by his wooden arms Anders let him fall as gently as possible into the abyss.

As the doll fell, a strange thing happened.

Anders had been too inexperienced to give the puppet more than an attempt at speech. He had been too short

of time to persevere, yet, as it fell, for a reason no one could ever account for, the poor creature cried out loudly and pitifully: '*Oh dear! Oh dear!*' as it dropped out of sight into the chasm. Its cry was so clear and penetrating that Anders expected every wooden soldier to come running to the spot. He dived head first into a patch of bilberries and lay there trembling from head to foot.

Fortunately for him only the nearest soldiers heard the puppet's cry. Thinking one of their companions was in some trouble they ran to the place and spent some time searching and prodding and peering down the crack and calling to their imaginary friend, while Anders' heart beat wildly as he expected every moment to be discovered. But the puppets soon gave up the search and went away.

Meanwhile Paul and Peterkin had heard the prince's cry of despair.

They thought the cry came from Anders. Either he had been captured by more of Malkin's soldiers, or he had fallen with his doll into the chasm. At this dreadful thought they stopped short in the middle of their dancing and broke into such sobs of misery and despair that the wooden soldiers were quite bewildered.

In vain they asked the twins to tell them what was the cause of their grief. Paul and Peterkin knew they must not speak and only sobbed more bitterly.

The soldiers offered all the consolation they could find. They held out sweetmeats and little presents and even wiped the twins' eyes with small white cotton handkerchiefs and patted them on the back with their clumsy wooden hands.

They were so long consoling Paul and Peterkin that none of the rest paid any attention to the prince's cry, which was very fortunate for Anders.

11

ELIZABETH

After some while Anders felt safe enough to look up from his hiding-place. All the soldiers had disappeared from sight.

Quick as a knife he leapt back to the boundary, where, with no doll to encumber him, he leapt over the rocks like a young deer. Safe on his own part of the Mountain he ran down the hill to blow a cheerful note on his horn that would summon the twins.

Their tears forgotten, they left the wooden soldiers staring, climbed the boundary with shouts of joy and galloped down the mountainside to join him.

'We quite thought you were dead!' they told Anders. 'And if you were not, we thought we would have to sing and dance for ever.'

They all went home with the news that they had done all that it was possible to do. The rest was left in Rudi's hands.

'How shall we know if he has made the key?' they pestered Anders during the evening.

'Why, the Mountain will come back to us, of course!'

'And when will that happen?'

'Why, when he has made the key, of course, you ninnies!' Anders said exasperated.

'Oh I do hope he makes it very quickly!' said the twins.

Their mother was so glad to have them safely home again that she kept them busy all the next day, so that they would not have time to go wandering up the Mountain.

Anders too stayed in the house. He looked solemn and serious, but old Peter Toymaker moved his chair outside into the sunshine for the first time for many days, gazing up at the Mountain as if at any moment it might change its course and begin to move back towards the village again.

The twins were so cheerful and full of optimism that the village people could not fail to notice their happy faces.

'Father will soon be home again!' Paul and Peterkin said when questioned.

'How do you know that?' their neighbours asked, but the twins shook their heads and had nothing to say.

'They have had good news!' the neighbours whispered to each other, puzzled, because Anders and Margaret still looked anxious and troubled, while old Peter Toymaker sat hour after hour gazing up the mountainside and shaking his head. Nobody knew what to think about it.

By now the people of Drüssl had lost all hope of keeping their Mountain. Some of them were making plans for changing their trades when the stock of pine trees came to an end. Others thought of leaving the village to go and live in the city. They seldom spoke of Rudi, even to each other, and kept their eyes averted from the Mountain.

When the sun began to set Margaret gave in to the twins' pleading and let them go out of doors to play.

It was so nearly supper time that she did not think of watching to see which way they went, nor asking Anders to keep an eye upon them. For once she had not even bound their fingers together.

Quick as rabbits the twins slipped out of sight behind the houses. If their mother called they would not hear her now. They trotted silently through the shadows towards the river bed.

They were almost convinced that by now their old friend the stream would be flowing again, and all the little fishes waiting for them, but the river bed was as wide as ever, the stones dry, the earth cracked and parched. On the far side wreaths of autumn mist swirled up the Mountain. The summit was out of sight.

'It hasn't come back!' said Paul.

'Father is a long time making the key!' said Peterkin with a sigh.

'He is taking a very long time!' said a voice at his elbow. There stood Elizabeth who had followed them unseen and was not in the least welcomed by her brothers.

'Go home at once!' they scolded her. 'You know Mother doesn't let you go out by yourself in the village! How dare you come after us?'

Elizabeth's lip trembled and she began to cry.

'Now we shall have to take her home!' grumbled Paul.

'And we can't go up the tunnel!' said Peterkin. Together they faced their little sister and said loudly: 'Elizabeth! You must go home! You must go home at once!'

Elizabeth turned back immediately, her chest heaving with sobs and tears running down her face.

'She's going!' said Paul.

'And we won't have to take her!' said Peterkin.

They hurried across the dry river bed to the foot of the Mountain, where Elizabeth, looking back across her shoulder, saw an amazing thing. Her two brothers stopped when they reached the further side and dived right inside the Mountain itself, where they completely disappeared from sight. She could hardly believe her eyes.

Elizabeth waited a long time to see them come back, but nothing happened and this made her more curious than ever. Whatever hole could have swallowed them up? She had heard much talk lately of tunnels and passages and great underground chasms but it meant little to her because she had never seen anything of the kind. But she felt she could not go home until she knew what the boys were up to, so she sat down on a stone where she was to watch for their return.

Nothing happened, and presently the church clock struck seven. Mother would be feeling anxious. She must go and tell Paul and Peterkin to come home.

She walked gingerly across the stony river-bed. How grim and dreary the place had become which had once been such a happy picnic spot! Often in the summer old Uncle Peter had come with them to the stream, where they sailed the pretty little boats that Father carved for them.

She stumbled across the shingle, filling her shoes with gravel and coarse earth, until she arrived where she had last seen her twin brothers.

Where they had disappeared tall ferns grew, but her sharp eyes were not long in discovering the hole behind them. Inside the entrance the tunnel was so dark she could see nothing, and there was no sign of the boys.

'Paul! Peterkin!' she called, but nobody answered.

By now she was frightened and felt she must find them if only to hold her hand and help her back across the river-bed.

'Paul! Peterkin!' she cried, venturing a few steps inside the tunnel, but there was no reply.

Instead, a pale, misty mountain light met her, lighting up her way. No longer so afraid, Elizabeth went forward, hoping to find her brothers round every corner.

Once, quite unknown to herself, she stepped across one of her own golden curls that the twins had dropped when carrying the coin, the ring and the scissors to Rudi. It lay across the tunnel like a golden barrier, flattened on the earth. Elizabeth had no idea of it.

Presently she had gone so far that she was afraid to go back, certain that her brothers must be close at hand.

She called their names, but all the answer she got was the ever increasing beat of the Mountain's heart – tick-*tock*! tick-*tock*! tick-*tock*! that grew so loud she could not even hear her own heart beating. Whatever could the strange noise be? She felt that whatever it was Paul and Peterkin would be there to explain it to her, so she went on, her breath coming short and fast, towards the tremendous

sound and the protection of her brothers until she had walked the whole length of the tunnel and came at last to the cupboard in the room where her father was a prisoner.

12

THE QUEEN AND THE PRINCE

When Paul and Peterkin were certain their sister had gone home they hurried up the tunnel to find out for themselves what was happening inside the Mountain. They longed to know how far their father had progressed in making the golden key, and whether the puppet prince had been discovered. How terrible if he were lying at the bottom of the chasm where they had dropped him, with his beautiful clothes all spoiled and dirty! What would happen to their father then?

Arrived at the cupboard they could hear voices talking against the giant thundering of the Mountain's heart. Father could not be making his key because he was not alone.

Peterkin put his eye to the crack and fairly jumped with excitement. Paul joined him, kneeling at his brother's side. The scene inside the ante-room kept them breathless as they glued their eyes to the crack that was their only peephole.

Rudi sat in his usual place looking pale and strained. His fingers opened and closed nervously and he seemed very restless and distracted.

Before him the doll-Queen stood, holding the puppet prince by the hand. He did not seem to have suffered by his fall but was as fresh and debonair as when Anders made him.

The Queen was demonstrating to Rudi how the little prince bowed and kissed her hands.

'*You* never treated me with such respect, Rudi!' she reproached him. 'Look how he worships me! But he cannot say a word! I am sure if he could he would pay me the most beautiful compliments! You never paid me any compliments, Rudi!'

'I came here against my will, madam!' Rudi repeated coldly.

The doll-Queen pouted.

'So did my little prince for that matter!' she returned. 'The soldiers found him lying at the bottom of the same chasm where they found you. He must have come there by accident as you did. But I never saw such a pretty little fellow in all my life. Malkin could not make anything like it. Just you wait, you rude and churlish Rudi Toymaker! Only three days more and you will be in Malkin's power – forced to be polite to me whether you like it or not! Once I had thought of making you my King! We could have got rid of wicked Malkin and ruled his kingdom between us, but you are so unkind to me I shall leave you here below and go up into the daylight with my little puppet prince, who will always do as I say.'

Rudi took no notice of her.

'Dance for me, little prince!' the Queen commanded.

The puppet prince danced a graceful movement, taking her hand and twirling her about with practised

ease. He finished with such a stately bow that one forgot
he was made of wood.

The twins, huddling inside the cupboard, were full of
admiration at the cleverness of Uncle Anders in making
such a masterpiece.

'Oh I do love you so much, my little prince!' the doll-
Queen cried. 'Now I am going to take you out into the
hall to introduce you to everyone! Farewell, you surly
old Rudi! I shall leave you alone with your sulks for
company!'

Tossing her head the doll-Queen swept towards the
door holding the prince by the hand. The twins were
about to bounce out of their hiding place when suddenly
the door was flung wide, right in the Queen's face, and,
brushing her aside, Malkin Toymaker strode into the
room.

The twins had never seen him before but no one else
could wear such an air of cunning malice and ill will.

Immediately, he noticed the puppet prince sheltering
in the Queen's skirts.

'What is that?' he demanded.

'The soldiers found him in the chasm!' the Queen
replied, folding her arms about her princeling. 'The
poor fellow had fallen from a great height and was
nearly knocked out of his senses! Don't tell me that
you made him, Malkin! for nothing will make me believe it! You have never made anything beautiful in
your life except myself, and I can grimace and squint
and leer and shriek as harshly as the best of them if I
choose to behave that way. I really cannot believe that
you made this pretty fellow!'

'*I* make him?' roared Malkin, snatching the puppet
out of the Queen's arms and holding it by the neck. 'Do
you think I would waste my time on a milksop like this?
A dummy? A ninepin? Pah!'

'But look how gracefully he stoops to kiss my hands!'
the Queen protested, 'and have you noticed his beautiful
clothes, Malkin?'

'Indeed I have! and I know who made them!' Malkin

cried in a fury. 'These were made by Elsa the dress-maker, sister to Rudi Toymaker here! I hear she now makes dresses for the Court and much good may it do her! She once made dresses for you, Marta, when she was poor, and glad to earn a penny or two to keep her wretched family!'

'I suppose Rudi had not won the King's prize in those days!' the doll-Queen said innocently.

Malkin snarled at her, examining the puppet. 'This wood – this carving – it came out of old Peter Toymaker's workshop I think,' he said thoughtfully. 'Old Peter's teaching perhaps, but not his own work. It is not Rudi's work either. There are careless slips here and there, like a boy's work – yes! I expect it was made by young Anders. *My* work indeed! this is a trick to deceive you, Marta, and I am ashamed of you, being taken in by the handiwork of a mere child! or was it the puppet's flattery that took you in? Mere vanity! Oh how piti-ful!'

'This is not the first time Anders has cheated me!' the doll-Queen cried, sobbing with humiliation. 'Once he tricked me into coming with him and tried to make me Queen of the trolls! Oh you hateful creature!' she shrieked at the doll-prince, seizing him by the leg and waving him wildly in the air. 'If I knock out your wooden brains it will be no more than you deserve!' And she flung him with all her strength across the room.

The puppet struck the cupboard door with a crash. The blow did not hurt him particularly, since he was entirely made of wood, but he thought it more prudent to remain huddled on the floor while the Queen was in such a rage.

It meant nothing to him that the blow had broken a panel in the cupboard door and that the anxious faces of Paul and Peterkin were peeping through.

13

THE TWINS ARE PRISONERS

The crash had come so suddenly that the twins never knew who first sprang across the room and pulled them out of the cupboard.

Their eyes were dazzled by the bright lights and bewildered by a crowd of people as they stood sobbing at their father's knee. Malkin stared at them in savage fury, Rudi in deep anxiety, and the Queen in curious delight.

'What adorable babies!' she cried, trying to enfold both of them in her arms together. 'Are these puppets too? No they cannot possibly be! The likeness is unmistakable! These are your own children, Rudi!'

The twins struggled away from her hard embrace, trying to go to their father, and at the same time Malkin strode across the floor to examine the hole in the cupboard.

'Just as I thought!' he said triumphantly. 'An entrance leading back to Drüssl! We must close it! The Mountain must move faster! The task is nearly finished, but the crack must be closed . . .!'

He bounded from the room to drive his puppet people to redouble their labours and soon a terrible vibration began, coupled with a creaking and a groaning. The beat of the heart seemed to hasten, while even at this depth the tremors that shook the Mountain could be felt.

In this new terror and anxiety no one noticed the face of little Elizabeth peeping through the gap behind the

broken cupboard door. They did not see her turn about, pale with fear and surprise, to run all the long way back to the tunnel's entrance, and then sobbing and stumbling, across the shingly stretches of the river-bed. Reaching the cottage at last she hurled herself into her mother's arms to pour out her story, of how the twins were held prisoner with Father in a hole inside the Mountain, guarded by wooden soldiers, and a beautiful lady with wicked eyes.

The whole family was stricken by this fresh disaster. Even the baby joined its wails to the general grief, when all of a sudden a sweet, muffled, far-off sound came to their ears from somewhere inside the room.

'The musical box!' Anders cried. 'It is singing inside the chest!'

He flew to open the lid.

The box was singing to itself without key or touch of human hand.

It sang:

> *'Be brave! Be brave! have courage!*
> *Love is a strong key*
> *And faith will turn it – turn it – turn it!'*

The singing box continued to sing 'turn it! – turn it!' more and more quietly until it finished, as if the spring had run down, until presently it stopped and sang no more.

The strange words had put fresh hope into their hearts. Margaret dried her tears and the baby laughed again.

'Malkin will have found the passage! He will close it and there is no other way for the twins to escape!' said Anders. 'I must go and warn the Mountain people. They may be able to help us.'

'Oh no, Anders! Not you too!' pleaded Margaret in despair.

'Remember what the musical box told us!' he said to her gently. 'Be brave! I shall come back again.'

He raced to the foot of the Mountain to summon his friend the chief troll. During the last few days the troll's face had become wizened with anxiety. He and his friends had stayed on the Mountain out of loyalty, but they had brought their treasures to the very foot, ready to remove them at the last possible minute.

'Our people are frightened to go inside the tunnel!' he told Anders. 'And the moment Malkin knows about it he will attack us from the other end. But we will do all we can to help you.'

He went off to warn his companions, while Anders climbed towards the boundary, anxious to see what was happening there.

The wooden soldiers were not even troubling to man their posts or to keep guard. They lolled about the rocks, chattering, but, even as Anders climbed, a tremendous vibration shook the Mountain, causing pine trees to uproot themselves and stones to avalanche, as, far below, Malkin drove his wooden slaves to greater efforts. The boundary slid whole feet down the mountainside, pushing boulders before it.

'Heavens! Is this the end?' Anders thought, clinging to the soil. Even the soldiers seemed afraid, rushing to and fro uttering purposeless shouts and cries.

But the shuddering died down till only a rhythmical trembling disturbed the earth. Anders hurried downhill – oh such a short distance now from Malkin's boundary! He found the trolls and goblins bravely propping open the tunnel's entrance with slabs of rock.

After a few grateful words of thanks he hurried home

to show his family that he at least was safe and sound, and they went to bed after praying for the safety of their dear ones, their hearts filled with hope for the morrow.

14

THE GOLDEN KEY

Deep inside the Mountain, Malkin continued to spur on his wooden people to work faster and faster. In between lashing them with his tongue and using all his magic powers he continually returned to the ante-room to see what progress was being made in closing the tunnel.

To his rage it did not appear to grow any smaller.

'It is so very far inside the Mountain!' the wooden soldiers told him. 'Maybe at the other end the entrance has already fallen in!'

'My people can move rock and earth and granite walls!' Malkin muttered to himself. 'What can prevent the tunnel from closing?'

With everyone preoccupied by the closing of the tunnel and the efforts of the puppet slaves no one noticed how Rudi's hand slipped inside his pocket, closed on something he found there, and began to twine and knead and twist it into shape. He was moulding the gold.

The great heart slowed to its normal beat as the puppets' efforts waned. They could not sustain the effort Malkin demanded of them. Their feet moved more and more slowly as they became exhausted.

'If the work is not finished by morning I shall burn you up, every one of you!' Malkin shouted, and the wooden puppets groaned, knowing how quickly they would perish, being made of wood. But they could do no more, and Malkin returned for the last time to the ante-room, pale with frustration.

The sleepy twins were longing for bed.

They were no longer afraid, because their father was there, and the beautiful lady was feeding them with cakes and sweets out of a silver dish.

'They must go to bed!' the doll-Queen said kindly. 'They are very young and need a full night's rest!'

But Rudi could not bear to let his children out of his sight.

'Don't be afraid!' the doll-Queen said. 'Neither Malkin nor his people shall harm a hair of their heads. Look! to prove that I am not deceiving you I will bind their hands together with silk, just as their mother does to keep them safe, as I can see by the mark on their little fingers. Oh you silly little boys to escape from such a safeguard! If you had obeyed her you would not be in Malkin's power today!'

For once Rudi trusted her, and felt she meant to do her best for the little boys. When she had tied together their little fingers he allowed them to be led away.

In the doorway they passed Malkin entering.

He was about to jostle the children when he sprang back – a look of terror on his face. He looked first at the protecting charm and then from Rudi to the Queen.

'Who did this?' he demanded. 'Why did you bodyguards allow it to happen?'

'It was the Queen's command. She did it herself, Malkin Toymaker,' the guards meekly replied.

The Queen swept from the room smiling triumphantly at Malkin, who was left muttering.

No mother could have put her children to bed with greater tenderness. Paul and Peterkin fell asleep on a silken couch, to the lullabies sung by the Queen. They could not be blamed for feeling that life in Malkin's country was quite pleasant after all.

But Malkin strode up and down the ante-room where Rudi sat, muttering and cursing.

'There is something wrong!' Rudi heard him murmur. 'What can it be?'

Suddenly he pointed to one of the wooden guards: 'Go down the passage and find out!' he commanded.

The sentry trembled with fear, but Malkin drove him
mercilessly into the cupboard. For a while the patter of
his feet could still be heard. Then silence. Time passed
and he did not return.

'Go after him!' Malkin shouted to a second and then
a third of his men.

Terrified, the little men scuttled into the cupboard
and disappeared. Too great a coward to follow them

Malkin stood at the entrance, fidgeting with impatience and peering into the misty tunnel beyond.

At last shuffling footsteps could be heard returning.

Two wooden heads appeared together, and the two last sentries climbed back into the room dragging the unconscious body of their companion. The little men were anxious and trembling.

'Something bars the corridor!' they said. 'Something that is made of gold! No magic power can move it! Our poor companion trod upon it and fell in a faint. We saved him but his feet are badly burned!'

'Take him to the hospital!' Malkin ordered. 'But what is this thing made of gold that resists all magic?'

'We have never seen it before, Master,' the puppets said humbly. 'But it looks like a lock of hair.'

'Then the tunnel must be guarded at either end!' Malkin commanded the rest of his guards. 'Send orders to the soldiers manning the boundary that they are to go down the Mountain and guard the farther end. I do not think there is anyone left in Drüssl brave enough to challenge them now. As for the rest of you! Guard this entrance with your lives! Remember that these children are now protected by a charm. They can walk between us and no power of ours can stop them. But if they see you and your muskets they may be afraid.'

The guards took up their positions beside the cupboard door. Rudi turned and twisted the gold in his pocket. Malkin faced him with an evil smile.

'As for you Master Toymaker, once of Drüssl,' he said, 'we won't raise your hopes by leaving you in a room with an open door! We must find you a new prison! Where shall it be? Ah! I have it! We will put you in the safest place of all – in the room where the heart of the Mountain beats! There you shall have the joy, in three days time, of hearing those heartbeats stop for ever! And once the Mountain is mine, everything upon it, yes, even the very heart of it, will be turned into stone!'

Rudi's own heart leapt with hope at Malkin's words. He could hardly have hoped for such a stroke of good fortune as to be shut in the very place where he must be to finish his plan. But Malkin must not suspect he had gold upon him or he would never allow him to go near the Mountain's heart. He took the greatest pains not to touch the wicked toymaker as they left the room together, passing through the hall where the workers toiled, through the three jewelled doors, right to the heart of the Mountain where it hung in space, beating its final heartbeats.

'People have been driven mad listening to it,' Malkin hissed in Rudi's ear. 'Perhaps you will be more willing to listen to me when the morning comes, for I have proposals to make to you. I mean in time to make you my chief Toymaker!'

Rudi kept scornful silence. The door banged to behind Malkin and he was left alone with the Mountain's heart. He could well imagine how men could lose their reason listening to the thunder of its beating, if they had nothing else to do. But for him it sounded a song of triumph and joy.

At last he was free to work out the charm that would save the Mountain!

He felt sure he could make and fit the key if he were left alone just long enough to finish it. How much of the three days and nights this would take he could not tell.

Taking the precious gold from his pocket he began to work.

All night long Rudi slaved at his delicate task, noticing the heartbeats as little as he had noticed the sighing of the pine trees near his home. He watched carefully for the doors to open but no one came until the guards brought his breakfast in the morning, when they found him lying apparently asleep on the floor, all traces of his work carefully tidied away.

Shortly afterwards the doll-Queen brought the twins, who wanted to see the heart and had been clamouring for their father. She seemed enchanted by the little boys, and could not stop fondling them or answering their persistent questions.

Rudi's impatience grew as they wandered about his prison, for every moment was precious when so many hours of work lay in front of him.

All the morning the Queen stayed beside the twins, playing games with them, stuffing them with sweets, treating them like a fond and indulgent mother. Rudi did his best to join in their games but Paul and Peterkin noticed his dejection.

'You play much better at home, Father!' they complained.

'Don't tease your poor father!' said the Queen. 'Just wait until Malkin makes him chief Toymaker! then you will see him happy again!'

At last the Queen was called away for a short while. Rudi at once called his sons to his side.

'You know what I must do!' he told them. 'Last night I began to make the key, but it is going to take me many, many hours to finish. By great good fortune I am shut up in the one place where I would hope to be, but how can I work with the Queen watching me all the time? Gold or no gold Malkin will find some way of spoiling my plans if he ever discovers what I am doing!'

'What shall we do, Father?' the twins asked anxiously.

'I want you to keep the Queen away from this room!' Rudi said. 'Pretend you are frightened of the heartbeats or that you want to explore the halls or talk to the soldiers. If I cannot have more time to work in everything will be lost.'

When the Queen returned she found the twins huddled dejectedly at their father's knee.

'We don't like it in here!' they whimpered when they saw her.

'We don't like the noise!' said Peterkin closing his ears.

'There is no room to run about in here!' Paul complained.

'Oh my poor little children!' exclaimed the doll-Queen, gathering them into her arms. 'I leave you for one moment and you become as miserable as your father! Come and see the beautiful birds I keep in silver cages, and the golden fish that swim in the fountain!'

When the twins were gone Rudi set to work again and worked for the rest of the day. The doll-Queen did not come back. Malkin never appeared. All night long he worked, yet the key advanced so slowly that he hardly dared to count the flying hours. He used every precious speck of the gold that had been brought him, each strand of golden hair, each grain from Margaret's ring, the golden scissors and the burgomaster's coin.

The key was of an intricate design. When he fitted the crude outline to the lock Rudi realized it still needed many hours to make it perfect.

By morning he was aching with tiredness but still working. His food was brought to him, but nobody came near him except the guards. He was able to hide his work from them by hiding it under his jacket.

He was constantly watchful for Malkin's coming, but the wicked toymaker was busy in the hall, urging forward his flagging puppets, while the twins had real stomach-aches from overeating on the day before. The doll-Queen was kept busy amusing them and consoling them in the absence of their mother.

A new atmosphere crept into the halls as if each puppet felt the approach of the end of their labours. The wooden sentries seemed suddenly alert and interested, brushing their uniforms and polishing their buttons in expectation of some great celebration to come. A weary joy lit up the wooden faces of the circling, trudging puppets in their endless march. Perhaps, after all, there would be a finish to their toil.

The heartbeats began very slowly to weaken, so slowly that at first no one noticed it. Tick-*tock*! Tick-*tock*! Tick-*tock*! Feebler and feebler it beat, while Rudi toiled feverishly, making the golden key.

15

THE BATTLE OF THE
WOODEN SOLDIERS

Anders' night was troubled by dreams.

Early in the morning he heard a light tapping at the door, and raced downstairs, expecting to find that the twins had escaped and found their way home. But on the doorstep he found the chief of the mountain trolls, carrying a spade, and apparently very anxious to get back to the Mountain.

'The wooden people are pouring down the mountainside!' he said in a hoarse whisper. 'They are swarming across the boundary, and we think they will make for the mouth of the tunnel. We mean to defend it with our lives, but first I came to tell you what is happening. I am afraid that in a few hours all entry to Rudi and your little nephews will be closed.'

Anders hastened to dress himself, and followed the little man as fast as his legs would carry him.

He did not arrive a moment too soon.

The trolls and goblins had taken up their positions at the tunnel's mouth, and were keeping watch in all directions, while above them could be heard the excited babbling of the wooden soldiers, the clatter of their feet descending the mountainside, and the clinking of their little muskets.

Anders was going to join his friends in defending the tunnel's mouth when he had a better idea. He leapt higher still to a cluster of rocks overhanging the entrance, that had once been a pretty waterfall, but was now parched and dry. Here he placed himself where he could reach some large boulders and stones that would make excellent ammunition, and seeing what he intended to do the trolls and goblins waved their hands joyfully from below, before retreating into the safety of the tunnel.

The little wooden men poured down the mountainside in a solid rush, chattering and screaming with excitement. They had just received Malkin's order to seize and occupy the entrance to the tunnel. They thought the campaign was over and the victory Malkin's, so they did not expect to meet the mountain people, thinking them fled a long time ago.

At the waterfall where Anders lay hidden the soldiers divided their ranks. Some ran down one side of it and some the other. None of them noticed Anders, who waited unseen, with a stone in either hand.

The wooden soldiers did not stop their headlong descent till they reached the river-bed, where they began a kind of war dance among the dry stones.

How stupid they are! Anders thought, as they passed the tunnel's mouth several times without seeing it. But at last one of the little men uttered a howl of triumph, pulling aside the swinging bramble that hid the entrance and displaying it to his friends. The next moment his shout turned into a yell of pain as one of the troll's spades fell heavily on his fingers. Malkin had succeeded in giving his men more sensitive feelings than Anders' puppet prince.

The rest of the soldiers hurried to the spot.

Bang! A dozen muskets went off before Anders could aim his first stone. But the trolls had placed a large boulder across the tunnel and the bullets bounced harmlessly off the surface. The wooden soldiers were poor marksmen. One even shot his companion by mistake. Anders saw the little man run off howling, to sit down at a safe distance where he could examine the splinters shot from his wooden leg.

Anders waited to release his stones, seeing that the soldiers intended to rush the entrance and drag away the boulder that shielded the trolls. They were reloading their muskets, preparing to fire them up the tunnel when it was free.

At the moment when they charged, Anders rolled his biggest rock upon them, following it with a shower of stones that bounded and catherine-wheeled down upon them, bruising wooden heads and hands, squashing fingers and toes.

There were cries of pain and anguish. A few muskets were discharged in the direction of the waterfall, but as they could not see Anders, the soldiers seemed to make up their minds it had been an accident. The wounded limped on one side while about half of the original number prepared to charge again.

Anders felt sure that the trolls could deal with this feebler assault by themselves, and sure enough the punishing clang and thwack of spade and shovel met the hands seeking to remove the stone. The puppets leapt backwards sucking their fingers, while peals of goblin laughter delighted Anders' ears. His one fear was that Malkin's people might launch an attack from inside the tunnel, but surely the mountain folk were too wise to be taken by surprise in such a fashion? He listened carefully for any cries of distress.

The Captain of the soldiers was calling for volunteers to seize the boulder, but as he led them forward in a fresh charge Anders sprang out of his hiding place and rolled rock after rock down upon them, caring little if he were seen, until the soldiers scattered in terror, taking shelter in any corner they could find, and firing their muskets wildly and ineffectively up the mountainside.

Anders could no longer reach them with his stones, and by their furtive movements he guessed they meant to creep round and surround him on all sides at once, which, if they were successful, would put him in the greatest danger.

Suddenly his fingers closed on something, inside his jacket pocket. It was his tinder box! – an old one that Rudi had given him for his own. It seemed as if it might save his life today!

As quickly as possible he began to tear up handfuls of dry grass and set them alight. Some tufts he threw down below him and others he scattered to left and to right. The little blazing handfuls set fire to the undergrowth, flames leaped upwards, flickered and flared, in a moment or two he was surrounded by a circle of fire.

The effect on the soldiers was instantaneous. Being made of wood they were terrified of fire. They fled for their lives on every side, howling and screaming, their only object to save themselves by getting back to the safety of their own boundary. Up the mountainside they scrambled, dragging their wounded with them, until their cries were lost in the trees above.

Anders laughed to see them fleeing. When they were gone he scrambled down to the tunnel's mouth, stamping out any smouldering patches he met on his way. The trolls and goblins, sheltering underground, came out to meet him, patting him admiringly with their hands and mopping the sweat from their wrinkled foreheads.

But the danger was not yet finished. The flames Anders had ignited were creeping up the mountainside.

If the pine trees were to catch fire then the Mountain would be as lost to Drüssl as if Malkin had captured it.

While they watched, however, a strange thing happened.

The dried-up waterfall where Anders had hidden, suddenly began to flow again. From deep among the long dried boulders the water welled up and fell in sparkling cascades. Rainbows danced across the tumbling drops. Tiny streams began to flow in all directions. They flowed downhill quenching the flames, that hissed and died, sending little coils of smoke spiralling into the air. The earth steamed, the fire died out, and when the scorched mountainside was cool again not a pine tree had been damaged.

Anders stared in astonishment, but the trolls and goblins seemed to take it for granted. They did not like to have their particular magic questioned or talked about, so Anders merely shook all their little brown hands and thanked them warmly for their help.

From the complete silence above it did not seem likely that the soldiers would resume their attack, but when Anders had been home for a brief visit to tell his family that he was safe and well, he built a fire on the river-bed and watched beside it for all the rest of that day and for the whole of the night.

16

THE KEY

The morning of the last day came. By evening the Mountain would be in Malkin's hands for ever, unless Rudi succeeded in finishing his key, which would change the beat of the Mountain's heart and bring it safely back where it belonged.

The key was nearly ready.

For the whole of a third night Rudi had worked, and there was only the final polishing to be done. Rudi hid it in a mousehole. His face was drawn with tiredness and anxiety. If the key were discovered now, after all his labour, he thought his heart would break, but there was no really safe place in Malkin's underground halls, because the puppet people were so sensitive to the presence of gold.

The guards had just brought his breakfast when Paul and Peterkin came in with the doll-Queen. Both were dressed in fine clothes like little princes. Their white tunics had scarlet facings. But they were sulky and restless, hanging back and unwilling to come into the room.

'I don't like these clothes. I like my own clothes best!' Paul said, fidgeting with his collar.

'Father doesn't want to see us anyway!' grumbled Peterkin.

'Not want to see his children dressed like princes?' said the Queen, showing them off with pride. 'Look how handsome they are, Rudi! Aren't you proud of your sons? Tonight they shall lead the procession with me through these gloomy halls, before we leave them for ever. Life above ground in Malkin's kingdom is very beautiful – haven't I told you so, my darlings? And you shall have everything you want in the world when I am Queen and your father is chief Toymaker. For sullen as he is,' the doll-Queen said with a sigh, 'I know he is the best Toymaker in all the world!'

The twins now sensed their father's impatience to get rid of them.

'We don't like it in here!' they cried.

'We don't like the noise.'

'We want to go out and talk to the soldiers!'

'We want to see the birds in the silver cages!'

'We want to feed the fishes in the fountain!'

'Take us away! We don't like it here!'

'Oh be quiet, both of you!' the Queen cried, losing patience with their clamouring. 'There, you see!' she added turning towards Rudi with a coy look that had no effect upon him at all. 'Your children do not want to stay with you. But *I* would like to stay and keep you company. Poor Rudi, how lonely you must be!'

Rudi did not seem to have heard. He turned his head aside and the doll-Queen flew into a rage.

'You should listen to what I say, Rudi Toymaker!' she stormed at him. 'Malkin is not to be trifled with! Your children are safe. They shall come with me to my kingdom and live like princes, but what about you? Unless you do as Malkin orders, a few hours after the heart stops beating you will be turned into stone!'

Rudi knew that he stood in great danger.

If he were prevented from finishing the key, if it did not fit the lock, then he would assuredly be turned into stone. In a few short hours he would know if he had succeeded. He faced the doll-Queen coldly:

'I will never work for Malkin Toymaker nor for any puppet of his,' he said firmly.

The doll-Queen stamped with rage.

'You will regret it!' she screamed. 'And your children will have a rock for a father!' She swept angrily from the room, pushing Paul and Peterkin in front of her.

Rudi at once set to work again on his key, polishing it as if his life depended on it, which indeed it did. Overhead the great heart beat ever more faintly. Now and again it faltered so that Rudi wondered if Malkin were ahead of his word and everything was over. At these moments his own heart throbbed so violently that he thought it must burst, but when it quieted down the heart of the Mountain was still pulsating feebly.

And at last, after a whole hour, the key was finished. It lay, small and perfect in the palm of his hand. Rudi knew that the workmanship was good, and now the time had come to try it in the lock.

Tiptoeing across the floor, Rudi listened. No one was coming. He took the key between his finger and thumb and walked resolutely towards the great heart. His hand trembled so much he nearly dropped it, but controlling himself sternly he pressed the tiny key into the keyhole.

It fitted perfectly. Rudi sighed with relief and thankfulness. All those weary hours had not been spent in vain! And slowly, firmly he began to turn the key inside the lock.

But it would not turn.

Rudi shook it, took it out and reversed it, coaxed it, rattled it, pressed and pushed it, all in vain. It fitted so perfectly he could not understand it. But although he tried it again many, many times, the little key would not turn the lock, until the shaft, bending in his hand, made him realize that it was not heavy enough!

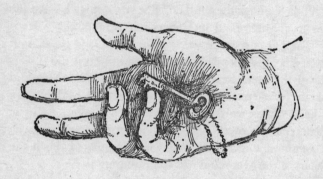

For the first time something like panic seized Rudi and filled him with despair. Why had not Margaret borrowed another coin? Why had the twins dropped one of Elizabeth's curls as they confessed they had done as they ran up the tunnel? How could he strengthen the shaft when all his gold was gone? But as Rudi's hand groped frantically from pocket to pocket they suddenly alighted on a tiny object that he had completely forgotten. It was the golden key of his musical box at home!

Snatching it from its slender chain Rudi set to work to

weld and knead it into the shaft of the key he had made. He had only six hours left to do the work.

Outside in the hall the twins were throwing themselves wholeheartedly into the preparations for the evening's feast. They were too young to be anxious, and felt sure besides, that their father would arrange everything to turn out well. So they teased the puppet cooks for samples of pastry and cakes, admired the new uniforms of the wooden guards, and watched the confectioners make an effigy of the Mountain in sugar, six feet high, covered with pine trees cut out in angelica and spun sugar.

The doll-Queen accompanied them wherever they wanted to go, delighted by their enthusiasm. She thought they were the most amusing playthings she had ever known, and gratified their slightest wishes. She hoped to keep them with her for ever and ever.

Malkin passed through the halls from time to time, giving orders and watching the preparations, a scowl on his face, since he had learnt of the defeat of his soldiers by the trolls and the goblins, but victory was so close at hand that this did not disturb him too deeply.

He had made his own plans for the future.

If Rudi would not submit to him and become his chief Toymaker he determined to destroy him as the doll-Queen had described. As for her, he intended to take away her powers little by little until she became a mere helpless doll again. She was becoming a great deal too powerful and the puppet people were beginning to defy Malkin in order to obey her. The twins would be sent home to their own village unless Rudi gave in, and wished to keep them with him.

These thoughts filled Malkin's head during the last hours of the Mountain's journey, quite unaware that in his prison below Rudi was toiling with every nerve and sinew to defeat his magic, while the moments fled away and in the banqueting hall the twins stuffed themselves with sugar plums.

By the sixth hour Rudi had welded the new gold into the key he had made. He was so engrossed by his work that he did not notice the silence gradually falling on the room, the patter of a mouse scampering across the floor, nor the clink of his own tools at work.

At the beginning of the last hour the heart's beat was no louder than that of an ordinary grandfather clock. Half an hour later it was no more audible than a wrist watch. It was then that Rudi raised his head.

But the heart had not quite stopped. And ten minutes later the key was finished! This time it *must* turn the lock! The shaft was stronger and firmer than before. Rudi refused to even think of failure.

But now there were footsteps in the passage outside with the sound of great doors opening and closing.

Hastily Rudi kicked his tools into the mousehole and hid the key in his coat. But it was only one of the guards come to clear away his dishes. The man looked up at the great heart.

'Quiet at last!' he said. 'Well it has thundered long enough! I'm glad to hear the end of it, that's what I say!'

He went out, carrying the dishes but leaving the door ajar, as if it were no longer as important to guard the prisoner as before.

Rudi sprang across the room to fit the key into the

lock. How easily it slipped into place! The new shaft was strong and well balanced, and needed only the slightest touch of a file to finish the work. This time it meant success!

The file was in the mousehole. Calmly and confidently Rudi went to fetch it, going down on his knees to pull it from its hiding place. But when he rose to his feet and turned round he found himself gazing straight into the face of Malkin Toymaker.

17

RUDI AND MALKIN

'Well Master Toymaker, what conjuring tricks are you playing on us?' asked Malkin, looking at Rudi's file and other tools that lay scattered round the mousehole. 'These look like a locksmith's tools. Did you expect to pick the locks and escape at this eleventh hour? Why take such trouble, my poor friend? Your village is ruined already and many of your neighbours are looking already for work in the city. Your wife and children will starve if they stay in Drüssl. Why not send for them to join you here and share your riches as my chief Toymaker? I shall ask very little of you in return. All your toys shall be of your own design and workmanship only they must bear my name as well as your own. We will be famous all the world over!'

Rudi's loathing of Malkin was so great that he could hardly speak. But it was so essential for him to have a few more moments to be alone that he choked back his feelings and said:

'Very well, Malkin, I will consider your offer. Give me just five minutes to think about your proposal and I will give you my reply.'

'I will come back in five minutes time!' Malkin said, with a gleam of triumph in his eye. 'And we will listen to the last beats of the Mountain's heart together, if indeed it has not stopped already!'

He made a movement towards the heart, and before Rudi could bar the way, his eye fell on the golden key, ready in position, waiting for the last grasp that would turn it in the lock.

Rudi sprang, but the Toymaker was quicker. With a scream that was half a snarl he thrust his black wand between Rudi and the dying heart, uttering a curse that turned Rudi's blood to water, so that his legs sagged beneath him and his file dropped out of his helpless fingers.

While Malkin's magic worked up and down his body like some terrible poison inside his veins, Rudi saw, as if in a dream, the room filling with wooden guards, summoned by Malkin's cry. He saw the Queen come in, her eyes wild and angry, followed by the wondering twins.

Helplessly bound by the spell, Rudi watched Malkin reach to snatch the key out of the heart, only to withdraw his hand with a terrible scream as the pure gold burned it. One by one the guards were ordered to try, but they too were defeated by the pain, and the Queen rushing in scornful fury to take it, cried out even louder than the rest of them.

'Bring me the key out of the lock!' Malkin ordered the twins but they calmly refused, and by the charm that protected them no one could force them to obey.

'No matter!' Malkin cried, regaining his wits. 'In a few more moments the heart will cease to beat. We have only to wait a little, for the end will come whether the key is in the lock or not.'

Half fainting under the power of Malkin's spell Rudi began to gather his forces together to resist.

'Turn the key!' he told the twins faintly. 'And if you cannot turn it, bring it to me!'

Neither Malkin nor his guards could prevent the twins, but they were too frail and small to turn the key, or even to remove it from the lock. Helplessly Rudi watched their struggles, while Malkin laughed aloud.

Rudi sank back in despair, and then with all the power and determination he had left to him he began to think of gold – of gold – of gold . . . of the gold pieces he had won as the King's prize for his singing box – of the burgomaster's gold chain worn at festivals, of the gold cross carried at church, of the golden sunrises and sunsets he had watched in other, happier days.

Little by little the terrible weakness left his limbs, his head cleared, his arms and legs felt strong again – his breath came deeply from his lungs.

And all of a sudden he sprang, surging like a whirl-wind on to the astonished Malkin, whose eyes and ears were fixed on the last feeble pulsations of the great heart whose dying murmur was all but gone.

Malkin tried to wield his wand again, but this time Rudi was proof against its power and knocked the blow aside. He defended himself as best he could, while the wooden soldiers clubbed and clouted Rudi from the rear and the doll-Queen tore at his clothes with tooth and nail.

Thinking that their father would be killed at any moment the twins shot out of the room, through the three great doors now standing wide, and into the ante-room, where they scrambled into the broken cupboard to bawl down the tunnel at the tops of their voices: 'Oh Uncle Anders! Uncle Anders! Come quickly to help Father, Uncle Anders!'

Down the long dark winding corridor the cry echoed, till a thin whisper of it arrived in the ears of the trolls and the goblins, and of Anders, keeping guard at the far end of it.

Meanwhile the battle in the hall of the Mountain's heart raged ever more furiously, with Rudi in the centre so beaten about and battered by Malkin, the doll-Queen and the wooden soldiers that he was in danger of being knocked senseless. And as they struggled he saw a smile slowly dawning on the wicked toymaker's face, a smile that could only mean one thing – the end was coming.

'Hold on, Rudi Toymaker!' Malkin shouted in triumph: 'Only fifty more seconds and you will have no more need to struggle! One – two . . . !'

Rudi launched a blow at every word that Malkin uttered, but his breath was coming in painful gasps, and he could hardly wrench himself out of the dolls' clawing hands, while the soldiers were clubbing him on head, back and shoulders with all the force of their wooden muskets.

'Twenty – twenty-one—!' shouted Malkin, and presently: 'Thirty-two! thirty-three! thirty-four!'

Suddenly a loud shout came from the doorway at Rudi's back. A well-known voice cried his name.

'Hold on, Rudi! Your friends are here!'

Smaller, shriller voices joined in. The clatter of picks and trowels joined the clash of the soldiers' muskets. Anders came bursting into the room at the head of a band of trolls and goblins, carrying flaring torches, and brandishing the golden curl by whose magic they had been able to force the narrow opening into the ante chamber.

The frightened puppets fled in all directions. Anders himself seized the doll-Queen as she clawed at Rudi.

'Miserable creature! What are you but a bundle of rags – a scarecrow!' he jeered. 'Who winds you up every morning, you poor plaything? Do you call yourself a Queen? If it wasn't such a joke I would pity you!'

He flung her carelessly into a corner where she lay sobbing helplessly, looking like any rejected doll.

'Thirty-nine – forty!' chanted Malkin, parrying Rudi's blows. Freed from other pressure the young toy-maker was able to put all the strength he had into attacking Malkin, who dodged and sprang and tried desperately to lure Rudi away from the heart into a far corner of the room.

'Forty-five!' Malkin's wand cut Rudi above the ear.

'Forty-six!' Rudi dived in with a blow that made Malkin stagger.

'Forty-seven!' Malkin skipped aside and tapped Rudi on the knee.

'Forty-eight!' Rudi's fist sent Malkin flying.

'Forty-nine!' In falling Malkin thrust out a foot to trip Rudi up, but leaping high in the air he cleared the wicked toymaker's body and reached the side of the dying heart.

With the whole of his strength he seized the key by the shaft and wrenched at it. If it broke now everything was over for ever. But if it turned . . .

And the key with a little tremble turned in the lock.

A tremendous quiet fell on them all. In the pause that followed Rudi wondered whether after all he had been just too late and under their eyes everything was now turning into stone.

But as they watched and waited the slightest breath of sound stole through the room, smaller than a bat's whisper or the brushing of two feathers in the wing of an owl. It was an infinitely brave and hopeful sound, the very beginning of the rebirth of time.

Tick-tock! *tick*-tock! *tick*-tock! It grew louder and louder until it was the tone of a normal heartbeat, louder and louder until one imagined the march of an advancing army. *Tick*-tock! *tick*-tock! *tick*-tock! It swelled louder and grander, beat by beat, until the whole room, the whole hall, the entire Mountain shook with it.

Once more the heart of the Mountain on its rightful course thundered down the arteries of its caverns, chasms and underground passages, while with a tremendous shuddering the roots of it withdrew themselves from the bonds that had held them in Malkin's country, and to the tune of its mighty heartbeats the Mountain travelled home.

Outside in the central hall the wooden puppets lay in piles of sawdust and shavings, the broken toys they were. Through their tangled ranks Malkin crept, a broken and wizened old man, to find some dingy corridor that would take him into his own kingdom. He led his limp and bedraggled doll by the hand. She too had shrunk from the dignity of a Queen to the size of a frail little child. Malkin was doomed to be an outcast, and watching him creep away, so small and old and unloved, Rudi could even find it in his heart to feel sorry for him.

18

THE MOUNTAIN COMES HOME

The news came to Drüssl from the children playing in the village street.

'The Mountain is coming back! – the Mountain is coming back to Drüssl!'

At the same moment the musical box in the chest began to play the most beautiful tune to Margaret, who was baking bread. Whatever were the words that it played they brought tears of joy into her eyes. She snatched up the sleeping baby and ran into the street where everyone seemed to be hurrying in the direction of the Mountain.

Old Peter Toymaker came limping after them, holding the hand of Elizabeth who skipped and shouted with excitement. Elsa was there on the arm of the burgomaster who helped her along. Every man, woman and child seemed to be in the street to witness the miracle that was happening to the Mountain as the pine trees came back to Drüssl.

On the banks of the stream the crowd stopped, quite astonished at what they saw. The air was warm and balmy, full of the hum of bees. Small woolly clouds, left over from the summer, blew along the Mountain's summit escorting her, as slowly and serenely she returned. No jars or tremors or earthquakes marked her coming. Like a galleon in full sail she advanced towards them, travelling across the breadth of the river-bed until the stony waste was covered again, the babbling brook flowed into its old channel, and the stepping stones emerged, cool and damp – a hiding place for a hundred fishes.

And still the Mountain moved.

Gently driving the stream, the river bank and even the villagers before it, like a goatherd his flocks, it travelled silently forward, to stop at last on the very edge of the village itself.

The whole of the Mountain had come to Drüssl!

As the Mountain came to rest they heard the joyful sound of a horn. From a shadowy hole under the water-fall appeared the head of Anders, followed by the twins, who raced into their mother's arms. Close behind them came Rudi himself, and at the sight of him the watching crowd raised a cheer that could be heard in all the mountains round as they saluted their Master toymaker, who had saved their Mountain and the livelihoods of the whole village.

That night was the happiest the family in the cottage had ever known. Rudi's adventures were told from beginning to end, and then the twins in turn told theirs. The singing box sang its most joyous tune, and then fell silent until a new key was made, after which it never showed any magical powers again.

A week after the Mountain's return the burgomaster gave a great feast in Rudi's honour. Rudi and Margaret sat at the head of the table with their sons beside them. Paul and Peterkin felt like heroes, but they were glad to have their little sister Elizabeth sitting between them.

Her courage had played a large part in their father's rescue and they were very proud of her.

Gradually life in the village of Drüssl settled down into its original busy and happy ways. The old trades flourished, and the twins became eager apprentices to their father, as soon as they could be trusted to carve without cutting all their fingers off. They could never forget the beautiful Queen who lived inside the Mountain, and it was their ambition one day to make a doll even more lovely than she, only this time she should be *good*!

On many a summer evening old Peter Toymaker strolled out-of-doors to look up at the Mountain overhead. He smelled the sweet strong scent of the pine trees that had made him his cradle and founded the trade he had taught to Rudi. The same trees would provide his coffin when his happy old age was done, and it did his heart good to know that even when he was no longer there the pines would still sigh and sing on the mountainside above the village, assuring the fortunes of generation after generation to come, and making provision for the age-old trade that had always been the livelihood of the toymakers of Drüssl.

Piccolo Book Selection

Piccolo Book Selection

True Adventures and Picture Histories

These and other PICCOLO Books are obtainable from all booksellers and newsagents. If you have any difficulty please send purchase price plus 7p postage to PO Box 11, Falmouth, Cornwall.

While every effort is made to keep prices low it is sometimes necessary to increase prices at short notice. PAN Books reserve the right to show new retail prices on covers which may differ from those advertised in the text or elsewhere.